TONY BRADMAN

WINTER
of the
WOLVES

BLOOMSBURY EDUCATION

LONDON OXFORD NEW YORK NEW DELHI SYDNEY

BLOOMSBURY EDUCATION
Bloomsbury Publishing Plc
50 Bedford Square, London, WC1B 3DP, UK

BLOOMSBURY, BLOOMSBURY EDUCATION and the Diana logo are trademarks of
Bloomsbury Publishing Plc

First published in Great Britain 2019 by Bloomsbury Publishing Plc
This electronic edition published 2019 by Bloomsbury Publishing Plc

A catalogue record for this book is available from the British Library

ISBN: PB: 978-1-4729-5378-0; ePDF: 978-1-4729-5377-3; ePub: 978-1-4729-5376-6

2 4 6 8 10 9 7 5 3 1

Typeset by Newgen KnowledgeWorks Pvt. Ltd., Chennai, India
Printed and bound by CPI Group (UK) Ltd, Croydon, CR0 4YY

All papers used by Bloomsbury Publishing Plc are natural, recyclable products from wood
grown in well managed forests. The manufacturing processes conform to the environmental
regulations of the country of origin

To find out more about our authors and books visit www.bloomsbury.com
and sign up for our newsletters

For everyone at ALCS

'Forþon ic mæg singan ond secgan spell…'
('So I can sing and tell a tale…')
— 'Widsith', sixth-century Old English poem

CONTENTS

CHAPTER ONE

Black Smoke, White Skull

The Land of the Angles (modern-day northern Germany), 525 CE

It took Oslaf most of the afternoon to bury his mother. The ground was hard on the hillside behind their farmhouse, and he wanted the grave to be deep. If it were too shallow, the wolves would be sure to dig her up, especially since autumn was turning into winter and there was less prey for them in the woods. She deserved peace after all her suffering, and he just couldn't bear the idea of what they might do to her.

He stopped digging when the sides of the grave were level with his shoulders, then set about pulling his mother into it. She was wrapped in an old cloak with only her white face showing and she felt lighter than air. The sickness had steadily sucked the life from her, leaving nothing but skin and bones. Oslaf wasn't tall for a boy of thirteen summers, but now she was smaller than him, like a child herself.

He placed her in the bottom of the grave and climbed out, only glancing down briefly before he started shovelling the soil back in. When it was full he piled rocks and stones on top to give her more protection. Eventually he turned to look beyond the farmhouse's thatched roof at the cold grey sea and the sky above it. A lone seagull circled slowly in the fading sunlight, squawking and mewing as if it were lost.

'Great goddess Friga,' said Oslaf, raising his hands, with the palms outward. 'I beg you to care for the spirit of my mother Leofwen on her journey to the Land of the Dead. We are not rich, so I have no fine clothes to bury her in, nor gold for her to take with her. But I promise that I will make a sacrifice to you when I can.' He put a hand on his chest. 'And you will be in my heart forever, Mother,' he said softly.

Oslaf wiped the tears from his eyes and walked down to the farmhouse. Inside, the hearth-fire had almost gone out and it took him a while to get it going again, blowing on the embers and feeding them with twigs. Once they were crackling, he sat on a bench and let the warmth soak into him, the familiar yellow glow of the flames pushing the shadows back to the corners of the room and up into the roof beams.

The farmhouse smelled stale from the days and nights of his mother's sickness. At first, desperately hoping that she would get better, Oslaf had only left her side to feed the chickens and check on the sheep in their pen. There had been just the two of them since his father had drowned the year before – he had gone fishing in their small boat and run into a storm. Oslaf's mother had never been the same after that. But then neither had he, come to think of it. He sorely missed his father.

The question was – what should he do now? He had no other kin who might take him in. His mother's parents had died before he was born, and his father had never spoken of any family. Oslaf had gone to the village to ask for help, but that had been a mistake. The people there had chased him off, and then a couple of days before his mother died, three men had come and stolen the sheep and the chickens and anything else they could lay their hands on. Oslaf had tried to stop them, of course, and eventually one of them had simply knocked him flat.

'Times are hard, boy, and we have families to feed,' the man had said, standing over him. 'Just give thanks to Woden and Thunor that we haven't killed you.'

That had been a bitter moment, one Oslaf would never forget. Now, as he sat alone in the farmhouse, he wondered about staying on

4

there. Maybe he could steal back the sheep and chickens, do some hunting and fishing to keep himself going. But even as he thought about it, he knew the idea was impossible. The villagers would kill him if he tried anything like that. And if even wolves struggled to live through the winter on what they could catch, he certainly wouldn't be able to – he'd starve before Yuletide.

He frowned, and stared into the flames. There was one place he could try... As she had neared her end, his mother had told him over and over again that he should ask Alfgar, the chieftain of a nearby village, to take him in. 'Alfgar is a strong chieftain, but he is a good man too,' she had said to him one night. She had been feverish, but she had come round long enough to say it one last time. 'Besides, his wife Elfritha and I were best friends when we were girls, before I met your father. Elfritha will remember me.'

Oslaf rose to his feet and went to stand by the door. The sun was setting behind the hill and darkness was filling the sky in the east. He knew he would have to follow his mother's advice, yet he could see no point in setting out this close to nightfall. So he closed and barred the door as they had always done, and made himself a bowl of porridge with a handful of stale oats that the men from the village had missed.

It was a lonely night in the farmhouse. Oslaf sat huddled beside the hearth, feeding the flames with the last of the logs, listening to the wolves howling hungrily in the woods. He tried to think of a better time, his mother sewing by lamplight while his father told them an old story. Oslaf's mother was an Angle, and a native of this coast. But his father was a Geat from a tribe across the sea, and they were great storytellers. Oslaf's favourite had always been the 'Tale of the Monsters from the Lake'.

He dozed off at last and slept badly, dreaming of monsters and his mother lying in her grave and his father's body sinking to the bottom of the sea. He woke just after dawn and decided not to drag things out – it would be best to get going quickly. The men from the village hadn't left him even a hunting spear or a knife, and he had nothing to take with him except the clothes he was wearing – his old brown tunic and trousers and shoes. After one last look round the farmhouse, he made for the door.

But there he paused. Suppose someone came to see if there was anything else left to steal? They would find an empty house waiting for them to move into…

Oslaf scowled at that thought. He strode back to the hearth and poked the embers with a twig to get the fire going again. Then he found the jar of resin-soaked rags his father had kept for making torches, and a piece of wood the right length. He wrapped a rag round the end of the wood and held it in the flames until it caught.

Moments later he was walking round inside the farmhouse, setting fire to anything that would burn. He went outside and ran the torch along the edges of the thatch, finally throwing it high up on to the roof. The flames took hold quickly, both inside and out, and soon they were greedily eating the whole farmhouse with a roar.

Oslaf walked away, a thick column of black smoke rising behind him.

Alfgar's village was a good two days' walk to the west, beyond the wide marsh that lay inland from the coast. Oslaf knew the marsh well and took the quickest route across it, sticking to the main track. A cold breeze from the east followed him, the tall reeds rustling as he passed between them, the marsh geese honking mournfully. They would be flying south soon, leaving the north before the winter came.

At sunset he reached the woods on the far side of the marsh, and spent an uneasy night trying to sleep in the branches of a tree. The next morning he left the woods and followed a stream that led through another marsh. He could drink from streams, but he had begun to feel hungry and was looking forward to reaching the next village. He hoped the villagers there would be kinder and give him something to eat.

The village, however, appeared to have been abandoned. Oslaf thought that was strange and he peered into the thatched log-houses, wondering where everyone had gone. They had left almost nothing behind, although he did find three withered apples in a pot that had been forgotten. He thought of sleeping in an empty house, but he didn't like the ghostly quiet of the place. So he passed another night in a tree, and late the next day he finally climbed a hill that looked down on Alfgar's village.

It filled most of a wide valley. Alfgar's hall was big, its walls made of oak logs, its thatch thick and grey like the bristling pelt of some giant wild boar. A cluster of houses huddled round it, a blue haze of woodsmoke from their hearth-fires hanging over them. The buildings were enclosed in a timber stockade, and outside it were animal pens and ploughed fields. Oslaf walked in through the open gates.

He followed a muddy track, marvelling at what he saw. The village blacksmith stood at the anvil in the hot red cave of his smithy, banging away with his hammer at the bent blade of a scythe. Elsewhere men and women went about their business: babies cried, children played, dogs chased each other, chickens squawked. Nobody seemed to take any notice of Oslaf. It was as if he were invisible.

He knew the hall would be the best place to find Alfgar, but he hesitated. The skull of a bull was fixed above the doors, its empty eye sockets staring down at him. Suddenly Oslaf felt afraid, his empty stomach twisting in on itself and making him wince with pain. If Alfgar turned him away he might just as well be dead…

Oslaf closed his eyes and tried to get his fear under control. He knew he shouldn't worry about what might, or might not, happen. The fate of everyone – their *wyrd* – was decided by the Three Sisters, the legendary Norns who sat at the foot of Yggdrasil, the Tree that Bears the World. The young hero in the 'Tale of the Monster from the Lake' had dealt with that by bravely facing every challenge. It was still hard, though, especially when you were completely on your own…

Oslaf took a deep breath, slowly let it out, opened his eyes – and crossed the threshold. It was dark inside the hall, although a fire burned in the hearth and oil lamps hung from the high roof beams. Long tables and benches stood against the walls, and Oslaf could just see a group of people at the far end, several men and boys and a woman. He walked on, heart pounding, and came to a halt in front of them.

They had been talking quietly, but now they all turned to stare at him. Oslaf guessed immediately which one was Alfgar, even though he had never seen him before. The chieftain was tall and broad-shouldered, his eyes blue and his hair and beard the colour of wheat just before harvest time. He was frowning, and he had the look of a man who was used to being instantly obeyed when he gave orders.

Oslaf had worked out what to say, going over it many times in his mind during his journey. 'Great chieftain, my name is Oslaf, son of Sigvald the Geat and Leofwen. They have both gone on their spirit journey to the Land of the Dead, and I beg you to give me shelter, warmth and food. This I ask before Woden and your people.'

'Don't listen to him, Father,' said someone from behind Alfgar. A boy a couple of years older than Oslaf pushed forward. He was almost as tall and broad as the chieftain and had the same colour hair, but his eyes were hazel. 'We can't take in every stray that turns up! We already have far too many mouths to feed.'

'He is not a stray, Wermund,' said someone else. The woman stepped forward, and Oslaf guessed she must be Elfritha. She also was tall, but she had raven-black hair, pale skin and dark brown eyes. 'My heart aches to hear that my old friend Leofwen is dead,' she said. 'There was a time when she and I were like sisters. You are more than welcome to stay here, Oslaf. Of course my husband and I will take you in.'

'Is that right, wife?' said Alfgar, looking round at her. 'It is good that you know my mind even before I do.' Elfritha met his gaze stubbornly, and he smiled. 'Yet we are as one in this,' he said. 'I will give you shelter, warmth and food, Oslaf son of Sigvald the Geat. But you will have to work for your keep – understood?'

Oslaf nodded, smiling too as relief flooded through him. Only one thing slightly spoiled the good feeling, and that was the sour look on the face of Alfgar's son.

But Oslaf decided not to worry about it – for the time being, anyway.

CHAPTER TWO

A Blind Old Fool

Elfritha made sure Oslaf was fed well that first evening, fetching him a bowl of lamb stew herself. There was good bread too, with plenty of sweet honey to spread on it, and a jug of ale to wash it all down. They sat in a corner of the hall, Elfritha watching him as he ate and drank. Alfgar and the others had gone, and the room was empty except for the two of them and an old man sitting on a stool by the hearth.

Oslaf glanced at the old man. His long hair and beard were white, but he sat upright and looked as if he had been strong in his youth. After a while Elfritha asked Oslaf if the stew was good, and at the sound of her voice the old man turned his head towards them. Oslaf saw then that he was blind, his eyes as milky-white as his hair. The old man listened for a moment, but said nothing and turned away once more.

'I should have guessed you were Leofwen's son,' Elfritha said. 'You're stocky like your father, yet your face and colouring is your mother's. When we were girls I was jealous of how brown her skin turned in the summer. Mine just burnt.'

Oslaf had never really thought about the way he looked, but Elfritha was right, he did have the same dark hair and eyes as his mother. Something else in what she had said interested him, though. 'Did you know my father?' he asked.

'Yes, I knew Sigvald.' Elfritha smiled. 'He and his friends were passing through, a bunch of young lads looking for adventure. Alfgar's father Aldhelm was still alive then and took a few of them into his war-band. Everyone could see Leofwen liked Sigvald, and that Sigvald felt the same about her. So it was no surprise to us that they got hand-fasted and went off together. Did they have happy lives?'

Oslaf had never really thought about that either, but now he did. His mind suddenly filled with memories of his mother and father laughing, and he realised that they had spent a good life in their little farmhouse by the sea. They had rarely paid much attention to what was going on in the rest of the world. His mother had always said they were enough for each other and needed nothing and nobody else.

'Yes, they did,' he said. 'All three of us were happy.' Until his father had died, he thought, and everything had changed. But he didn't say that.

'Well, I am glad to hear it,' said Elfritha, smiling. 'And I hope you will be happy with us, Oslaf. But Alfgar was serious when he talked about you earning your keep. My son was right, we have taken in others, and we have many mouths to feed. So there is no room here for those who will not work – we all have to pull our weight.'

Oslaf found his eyes drawn again to the old man, and was surprised to see he was smiling too. 'I know what you're thinking, boy,' said the old man, his voice rich and deep. 'A blind old fool like me can't do anything useful. Probably best to let the wolves have me, wouldn't you say? Although there's not much meat on my bones these days, and what's left might be too tough even for a hungry wolf pack.'

'I… I wasn't thinking that, truly I wasn't…' Oslaf spluttered, taken aback. The old man's words were something of a shock. Oslaf had not expected him to speak, or even to know that he was being looked at. But he had instantly sensed Oslaf's gaze – and had known much of what was in his mind. 'Not the part about giving you to the wolves, anyway,' Oslaf said. 'But I did wonder what work you might do.'

'At least you are honest,' said the old man. 'I do the most important work of all. I am Lord Alfgar's wordsmith, his praise-singer, his teller of wondrous tales…'

'Or to put it more simply, Widsith is our poet, our *scop*,' said Elfritha. 'Poets can be irritating, mostly because they're so vain. But every hall should have one.'

Oslaf had heard of *scops* before, so he knew a little about them. His father had told him how respected they were among the Geats, and how the best were sought out by great chieftains and princes. He looked at the old man rather differently now.

'Quite right,' said Widsith, laughing. 'You will see how useful I can be, boy.'

'But not tonight,' said Elfritha. 'I think Oslaf needs rest after his journey.'

It was true; he could hardly keep his eyes open now that he had eaten. Elfritha showed him to a place at the far end of the hall where he could sleep and gave him some furs to keep him warm. He lay down and darkness swept over his mind.

He was woken early the next morning by Beornath, Alfgar's steward, the man who was charged with running the village in the chieftain's name. Elfritha had warned him that Beornath would be coming, and Oslaf recognised him as one of the men who'd been with Alfgar the night before.

Beornath the steward was short and broad, with plenty of thick black hair on his cheeks and chin but not much on his head.

'Up you get, boy,' he said, standing over Oslaf. He turned and walked off, and Oslaf jumped up to follow him, pulling on his shoes and nearly falling over.

Beornath was waiting for him outside. 'So then, what can you do?'

'Most things that need to be done on a farm,' Oslaf said nervously.

'Really?' said Beornath, looking him up and down. Clearly he was not very impressed. 'We'll see about that, won't we? You'd better come with me.'

Beornath told him to start by chopping some firewood, a job Oslaf had always enjoyed. There was something satisfying about swinging the axe down and the *thunk* it made when it hit the wood, which split cleanly if you did it right. His father had also taught him how to stack a woodpile so the logs stayed dry and were easy to get at. It was a bright day with a chill in the air, and the work kept him warm.

Next Beornath got him to clean out one of the pigpens, which meant persuading a large, grumpy old sow to move to another. That was easy enough – Oslaf knew he just had to show her who was master. And finally Beornath took him to a small field outside the stockade to help a group of men and women sowing winter wheat, casting the seeds into the ploughed furrows. Oslaf had no trouble doing that, either.

'I suppose you'll do,' said a smiling Beornath when the work was done. 'Go to the hall and get yourself something to eat. I'll have more tasks for you later.'

Oslaf nodded and headed back into the village, pleased that he seemed to have made a good start in his new life. For a few moments while he had been working he had almost forgotten that he had buried his mother only a few days before and was a stranger in this village. Now he prayed in his heart to Woden, asking the god to watch over him, to make sure he chose the right path in the days to come.

'Hey, where do you think *you're* going?' somebody said behind him.

Oslaf had reached the hall and was about to pass through the doors. He turned round to find out who had spoken and saw Wermund looking at him. Alfgar's son was wearing a fine green tunic and black trousers tucked into good boots. A blade in a leather scabbard hung on his belt. It was a *seax*, the long knife favoured by the Angles, and a good one too, with an ivory handle and a silver pommel.

There were half a dozen boys with him, and Oslaf realised immediately they looked to Wermund as their leader. A couple were as young as Oslaf, but the others were much the same age as Wermund or even a little older. Now Wermund walked up to Oslaf and stood in front of him, hands on hips, his eyes narrowed. Oslaf had to look up to meet Wermund's gaze – the older boy was half a head taller.

'Er… Beornath told me to come to the hall for something to eat,' said Oslaf.

'Did he, now?' Wermund said, nodding. 'Well, you clearly haven't learned your place here yet. Oh, I know your mother was my mother's friend, but that counts for nothing with me. I'm guessing you have no other kin, or you wouldn't be here. So that means you're not worthy to enter my father's hall through the main doors. There is another door at the rear for people like you, the servants and slaves.'

'I am freeborn,' Oslaf said quietly. 'I have the right to go where I want.'

'Not if I say you can't.' Wermund poked a finger into Oslaf's chest. 'I am the firstborn son of Alfgar, lord of this hall, and I will decide what you can do.'

Oslaf felt a hot wave of anger flood through him. Why was Wermund treating him this way? He had simply asked for shelter and Wermund seemed to hate him for it. Now Oslaf clenched his fists… but then the voice of Woden seemed to speak inside his head. *This is not the time*, the god said. *The odds are stacked against you… wait until things are more in your favour.* Oslaf knew it was good advice, so he silently thanked Woden – and stood aside.

'Fair enough,' he said with a shrug, his eyes fixed on Wermund's.

'I'm glad you think so,' said Wermund, holding his gaze. Then he smiled and went into the hall, the other boys ignoring Oslaf as they followed their leader.

Oslaf turned and walked away, still angry, wishing now that he had never come to Alfgar's village. He hated the way Wermund had humiliated him in front of his followers. Perhaps he should tell Elfritha how her son had just behaved… though that would probably make things worse. Elfritha had been very good to him, but Wermund was her son, so she was bound to take his side against a stranger.

Oslaf didn't think about where he was going. He walked past houses and people, taking no notice of anything or anybody. After a while, he realised he had come to the village gates. They were open and he went through them. Widsith was outside, sitting on a small stool in front of the stockade, his lined face lifted to the warmth of the autumn sun. He heard Oslaf's footsteps and turned towards the sound.

'Leaving us already, boy?' Widsith said, smiling. 'You didn't last long.'

How did the old man know it was him? Oslaf was less surprised this time, but it still felt strange, even a little magical. Perhaps Widsith was a sorcerer as well as a poet, Oslaf thought, and shivered as if someone had just walked over his grave.

'Believe me, I would if I could,' he said. 'But I have nowhere else to go.'

'Well, that's as good a reason to stay as any,' said Widsith. Suddenly he tilted his head to one side, like a hound who has heard something. 'Ah, here they come.'

'Who?' Oslaf peered up the track out of the valley. 'I don't see anybody.'

'You will soon,' said Widsith. 'Alfgar sent out half a dozen of his warriors three days ago to scout towards the east. And now they return. Let us hope the news they bring is good.'

Then Oslaf could hear it too, the soft thudding of hooves and the jingle of harnesses. At last a group of helmeted men on horses came riding down the track. So these were warriors, thought Oslaf. There had been many descriptions of such men in his father's tales, but Oslaf had never actually seen a real one. Some wore leather jerkins covered in metal plates, while others were in chain mail. Each man had a *seax* on his belt and was carrying a spear. Their round wooden shields – all of them painted in strong colours: red and blue, yellow and green – were slung over their backs.

'Bright and burnished were their weapons, brave the men,' Widsith chanted as they rode into the village, his voice taking on a strange, haunting quality. 'A lord always needs plenty of good warriors to serve him,' he added in his normal voice, smiling once more. 'As well as a great *scop* to sing his praises, of course.'

Oslaf stopped listening, unable to take his eyes off the warriors, watching them till the last horse's tail vanished with a flick inside the village gates. It was almost as if Woden was speaking to him again, or perhaps it was Thunor, god of thunder. Whoever it was seemed to be saying: *you have just seen the answer...*

It was clear to Oslaf now – he would become a warrior.

He smiled, and hurried back in through the gates.

CHAPTER THREE
First to Draw Blood

The more he thought about it over the next few days, the more sense it made. Oslaf looked around him to see what people actually did in the village, and he quickly realised that everyone helped out with the farm work. Many were possibly better at some things than others, but they could all – men, women, even the children – turn their hands to most tasks. Being a warrior, however, was very different.

They had a special name, for a start, one Oslaf had heard before. In his father's tales, a lord's warriors, his war-band and personal bodyguard, were called his hearth-companions. According to Widsith, Alfgar had fifty such men. Each had taken an oath, swearing to be faithful to his chieftain and to fight to the death for him and his shield-brothers, the other hearth-companions. Of course, they were also members of the tribe – which was known as the *Alfgaringas*, after the chieftain – so they were sons and husbands and fathers too. But loyalty to their lord always came first.

'Their lord has a duty to them as well,' said Widsith one evening. Oslaf was sitting beside him in the hall. It was something he had taken to doing – he enjoyed listening to Widsith, and he got the feeling that Widsith liked having him around. 'He swears to be a good leader and a ring-giver, a lord who fights in the front rank in battle and brings them honour and glory and treasure. Weak lords lose their warriors, strong lords draw good men to them. Alfgar is a worthy lord. His hearth-companions would walk barefoot through fire if he ordered it.'

And that same evening Oslaf finally heard Widsith sing. The whole village had gathered in the hall for a feast and to hear a tale or two from him. Everyone came in their best clothes and sat at long tables, eating and drinking and laughing – Oslaf had never heard such a noise. He sat where Elfritha said he should, at the high table with her and Alfgar and their children. Wermund had a sister called Gunnhild, who appeared to be much the same age as Oslaf. She was fair like her father, but had her mother's dark eyes.

Gunnhild smiled at Oslaf as he sat down, but Wermund scowled. 'Why is *he* sitting with us, Father?' Wermund said, nodding crossly in Oslaf's direction. Oslaf stayed silent, yet kept his head up and tried to look as if Wermund's words meant nothing to him. Alfgar sighed and turned to answer his son, but it was Elfritha who spoke.

'Be quiet, Wermund,' she said. 'Widsith is about to start singing.'

Wermund puffed out his cheeks, but said no more. The hall fell silent, everyone gazing at Widsith. The old *scop* was sitting on his stool by the hearth-fire, but he had swapped his usual tunic for a long robe of fine white wool. He held a small harp on his lap, the strings glinting in the light from the fire and the oil lamps hanging from the roof beams. He waited for a moment, then struck an opening chord.

'Hear me as I unlock my word-hoard!' he said, and his voice rang out clearly around the hall. 'I sing of a bold hero, blades clashing, blood and gold…'

It was a thrilling tale, the story of a young warrior fighting for a chieftain in a faraway land, and Widsith told it brilliantly. Just like everyone else in the hall, Oslaf was entranced, gripped by the twists and turns of what happened, worried for the hero when he was threatened, relieved when he got out of trouble, cheering along with the people on the benches around him when he killed his deadliest enemy after a long, bitter duel.

By the time Widsith struck the last chord, Oslaf wanted more than ever to be like the hero. It was clear a great warrior would always find a home in the hall of a worthy lord. Although how did he go about becoming a warrior here? He prayed to Woden once more, and to Thunor, asking them to show him the path that would lead from what he was now – a kinless boy who had been taken in, but who had no certain place – to becoming one of Alfgar's trusted men, a hearth-companion.

To his surprise, the gods answered his prayer the very next day.

It was late in the morning when Beornath sent Oslaf to help with the stacking of the hay, which was being stored for winter feed, in one of Alfgar's barns. The village was a little slow getting started that day – it seemed a lot of people had drunk too much mead the night before and had woken with sore heads. Oslaf felt fine, although he had found it quite hard to sleep, his own head full of the scenes conjured up by Widsith's tale.

There was a large open space beside the barn, and Oslaf saw it was occupied by a crowd of boys armed with shields and short spears. They were fighting in pairs, jabbing the spears at each other, the blades clunking on the shields. Three of Alfgar's hearth-companions looked on, calling out instructions and comments. Oslaf walked over and stood beside the men, trying to summon up the courage to speak.

'Please… can I ask what they are doing?' he managed to say eventually.

'They are learning to be warriors,' said one of the men without taking his eyes off the boys. He was tall, dark and broad-shouldered, and had a jagged white scar that ran down the side of his neck. Oslaf knew he was called Tovi, and that he was Alfgar's second in command. 'At least that's what they're supposed to be doing,' Tovi said, and sighed. 'In Thunor's name, Ottar, keep your shield up…'

'Can I join in?' asked Oslaf nervously. 'I want to learn how to be a warrior.'

Tovi turned to look at him. 'You're the boy Alfgar has just taken in, aren't you?' he said. Oslaf nodded and held the man's gaze. Tovi smiled at last. 'Well, I don't see why not,' he said with a shrug. 'Find the lad a shield and a spear, Ragni.'

One of the other two men gave Oslaf a shield and a spear from a few that were stacked against the wall of the barn. The third man – whose name was Bebba – showed Oslaf how to slip his left arm through the leather straps on the back of the shield. It was heavy, but felt good, which was strange. Oslaf had gone hunting many times with his father, so he had often handled a spear. Yet he had never carried a shield before, not unless he counted the toy his father had made for him.

'I don't believe it!' somebody yelled suddenly. 'What are *you* doing here?'

It was Wermund. He angrily pushed his way out of the crowd of boys, holding his shield and spear as if he were about to go into battle. 'You can't train with us,' he added, practically spitting the words at Oslaf. 'I won't allow it, do you hear?'

'But I will,' Tovi said. 'Unless you can give me a reason, Wermund.'

'A reason?' said Wermund. Tovi stared at him. 'I just don't think it's right,' he said, his cheeks turning red. Oslaf could see he didn't like having to explain himself. 'He's… well, he's not one of us…'

'Really?' said Tovi. 'But your father has willingly taken him in. And now he is warmed by the same hearth-fire as you, and eats the same food and sleeps beneath the same roof.'

'That may be so, but…' Wermund began, looking round for support. None of the boys spoke up for him, however – it was clear they were scared of Tovi, and Oslaf could see why. The warrior seemed friendly enough, but there was a powerful sense of menace about him as well. 'What I mean is that we don't need somebody like him to fight for us, somebody without any kin…' Wermund finished lamely.

'You're wrong about that, Wermund,' said another voice. Everyone looked round and saw Alfgar striding towards them. 'In times like these we would be fools if we turned away anybody willing to help us fight our enemies, even those without kin. There are always new tribes, new peoples coming from the east to take what is ours. The only question to ask is: does this boy have the courage to face the storm of battle?'

'I do, Lord,' said Oslaf. 'Please, give me a chance to show you.'

'That's easily done,' Wermund snapped. 'Let me fight him, Father.'

Alfgar stared at his son with narrowed eyes, then slowly shifted his gaze to Oslaf. The tense hush of before deepened now. It seemed to Oslaf that everyone was holding their breath while they waited to hear Alfgar's reply. The chieftain turned at last to Tovi, who looked at him and shrugged once more, as if to say – *why not?*

'Very well,' said Alfgar. 'At least that way we'll find out if the lad has any courage. And if it keeps my son quiet, then so much the better. You had better explain the rules, Tovi.'

'Can't we just get on with it?' said Wermund. 'I know the rules.'

'Be patient, Wermund, your opponent might not,' said Tovi. 'Both of you will strip to the waist and fight inside the marked square. If you are pushed out of the square, you lose. If you deliberately step out of the square to gain an advantage over your opponent, you lose. If you drop your spear, you lose. The winner will be the first to draw blood. And try not to kill each other, lads. This is not a duel to the death.'

The rest of the boys had instantly become excited, a buzz of anticipation running through them. Wermund was quickly surrounded by his friends. They helped him to pull off his tunic and checked his spear and his shield, making sure the straps weren't too loose or too tight. Others marked out the fighting square, twenty paces on each side, scoring straight lines in the soil with the tips of their spear-blades.

Oslaf felt sick. His stomach churned and his heart pounded as if it were about to burst out of his chest. He felt terribly alone too – but then Tovi came over to him.

'Give me your shield and spear,' Tovi said. Oslaf did as he was told, shivering as he felt the chill air touch his skin. Tovi helped him take off his tunic, then gave him back his spear and shield, leaning in close to adjust the straps. 'He will come hard at you, and try to knock you out of the square,' Tovi whispered. 'Make sure you stay in the middle, keep your shield up – and watch his eyes, not his spear.'

Oslaf glanced at the man. Tovi winked, gave him back his spear, then led him over to the nearest side of the square. Wermund was waiting on the other side. Boys jostled with each other, struggling to be at the front. They laughed and cheered and called out, making bets on how swiftly Wermund would win. Oslaf forced himself to take no notice, concentrating instead on looking into Wermund's eyes.

'May Thunor give victory to the best man,' Tovi roared. 'Let the fight begin!'

Oslaf said a silent prayer to Woden and stepped into the square. Wermund sprang forward and smashed his shield into Oslaf's, trying to force him out of the square before the fight had properly begun. Oslaf, however, remembered Tovi's words and dug his heels in, holding to the middle. Wermund scowled and stepped back.

'Come on, Wermund!' somebody yelled. 'You should have won by now.'

Wermund hunched behind his shield, his eyes only just visible above the rim. He crouched a little, holding his spear high and pointing the blade downwards, and Oslaf did the same. The next attack came soon enough, Wermund moving quickly, his spear-blade flicking at Oslaf like the tongue of a snake. Oslaf kept his shield up and dared a thrust of his own, aiming at Wermund's right shoulder and just missing.

Wermund looked startled, and the crowd cheered again. The two boys moved around the square, jabbing with their spears, Wermund pushing and probing, Oslaf sticking to Tovi's advice and gaining confidence. But soon Oslaf's shoulder ached terribly, and he lowered his shield – which left his face exposed.

Wermund took his chance, his spear-blade flicking forward and slicing into Oslaf's cheek. Oslaf reeled back, hot blood springing from the wound and dripping off his jaw. He glanced at his opponent, their eyes meeting, and for the briefest of instants he thought Wermund seemed shocked, perhaps even guilty at what he had done.

'Hold!' yelled Tovi. 'I declare Wermund, son of Alfgar, the winner!'

The biggest cheer of all went up now, and Wermund's face hardened into a mask of triumph. He banged his spear-shaft on his shield, and grinned as he accepted the acclaim of his friends. Then Alfgar stepped forward and silence fell again.

'You did well, my son,' Alfgar said. 'But so did you, Oslaf, even though you lost. You have earned your place with the boys. Elfritha will see to your wound.'

Oslaf was pleased and smiled, although it made his cheek hurt even more, and Tovi slapped his back. 'You'd have won if you'd kept your shield up…' he said.

But Oslaf wasn't listening. Wermund was staring at him through the crowd with a look of pure hatred, and Oslaf had a feeling that the real fight between them had only just begun.

CHAPTER FOUR

Winter of the Wolves

'You'll have a scar, but I don't suppose that will worry you,' said Elfritha, who was the village healer. They were in the hall, Oslaf sitting on a bench with Elfritha and Gunnhild. The blood had stopped flowing from his wound, and Elfritha had cleaned his cheek with a cloth and warm water from a bowl Gunnhild was holding. 'I know what you boys are like,' Elfritha went on. 'You think a scar gives you the look of a warrior.'

'I will try not to be so foolish, lady,' Oslaf replied. 'My mother always used to say that a scar should be a lesson learned. And I am grateful for your care.'

'It seems Leofwen grew wise as a mother, and passed on her wisdom to you,' said Elfritha. 'How I wish she were here to give me her counsel!' She sighed and shook her head. 'I am sorry Wermund did this to you, Oslaf. He has his moods, and recently he has become... difficult. Perhaps I should speak to him for you.'

'Please don't,' Oslaf said quickly. If Elfritha got involved it would simply make him look weak. He knew that he would have to deal with Wermund himself.

'Well, if you're sure...' said Elfritha. Oslaf nodded, and she rose to her feet. 'Let me know if the wound starts to bleed again – I can always seal it with a spider-web poultice.' He watched her walk off, and felt grateful to her all over again.

'It's true, my brother has changed,' said Gunnhild once Elfritha was out of earshot. 'He never used to be the way he is now. It seems that he cannot stand to be thwarted, and he loves to lord it over the other boys... I asked Mother if he might have been taken over by some evil spirit. But she believes he is just impatient to be a man and win glory and honour, and that he needs careful handling for a while.'

'I'll bear that in mind,' said Oslaf. He touched his cheek, and winced.

'I'm glad to hear it,' said Gunnhild with a smile. 'I wouldn't want to see you getting hurt again because of him. We're not all horrible in my family.'

Oslaf smiled back, and felt pleased for a second time that day.

It seemed he might actually have a friend in Alfgar's hall.

Oslaf grew used to living in the village, the rhythm of the days from dawn till dusk, the evenings in the hall by the hearth-fire, talking and resting. There were times when he thought of his father and mother and a terrible sadness filled him, and he thought his heart might break. Then he would pray to Woden, asking the god to watch over his parents in the Land of the Dead, and gradually the feeling would pass.

He loved the training he did with Tovi, though. The boys worked hard with spear and shield, and sometimes Tovi let them try an axe or even a sword. Tovi didn't say much in the way of praise, nodding occasionally if he thought a boy had done something particularly well. Oslaf soon became desperate to win one of those nods, and on a day when he got two or three he felt very pleased with himself.

Wermund was clearly the best of them all and liked to challenge the others. Oslaf steered clear of him, remembering what Gunnhild had said, and Tovi made sure they were never paired together. Yet there was still tension between them, and Wermund took every opportunity to mock Oslaf – although only when Tovi couldn't hear him. Oslaf tried to shrug it off and concentrate on whatever he should be doing.

One cold, damp, blustery day, when the sky was full of thick clouds and a chill wind was blowing from the north, Oslaf saw half a dozen hearth-companions led by a grim-faced Tovi ride back into the village and up to the hall. Tovi jumped off his horse and marched in through the great doors. Oslaf was curious and followed him inside, then watched as Tovi said something that made Alfgar frown deeply.

Alfgar drew Tovi into his private chamber at the rear of the hall and pulled the deer-hide curtains closed behind them. Oslaf felt uneasy, wondering what Tovi had said to make a chieftain with fifty spears at his bidding look so unhappy.

'It seems that Tovi has brought us bad tidings,' said Widsith, who was sitting in his usual place at the hearth-fire. Oslaf walked over and sat down beside him.

'What is going on?' he asked. Oslaf took it for granted the old man would have been able to hear everything that had just been said, even though Tovi and Alfgar were whispering.

'Tovi saw a big war-band, outriders of yet another new tribe that has decided to try its luck westwards,' said Widsith. 'They will pick the land clean, attack any villages they come across, and leave a trail of fire and blood and death in their wake…'

Widsith talked on, skilfully weaving a tale of the past and the present as only he could. Now Oslaf understood why the village in the marshes had been abandoned. Its people had simply grown tired of fighting off new tribes and gone to live somewhere else.

'Why then has Alfgar not led his people to another place?' said Oslaf.

'Alfgar is stubborn. This is his land and he will not give it up lightly. He is strong too, and he knows how to fight, which is why others come to him and ask to be taken in when their villages are burnt down. But it gets harder every year… each new tribe says there are other, bigger tribes that forced them out of the east.'

'So where do people go when they leave their homes?' said Oslaf. He had little idea of the world beyond the coast, the marshlands and now Alfgar's village. His father had often talked of the land of the Geats, and he had mentioned other strange places in the stories he told. But none of them had ever seemed real to Oslaf.

'Westwards, always westwards,' said Widsith. 'Most cross the great River Rhine into the rich lands that used to be ruled by the Romans – Gaul, Hispania, Italy. That's where the Franks went, and the Goths and the Vandals. I travelled in those lands before I went blind, and I saw such marvels – ruined villages of houses built from stone, shining halls where it seemed the gods themselves had once lived…'

Oslaf struggled to picture in his mind such wonders. He thought Widsith had probably made them up – after all, that was the kind of thing poets did.

'But what about our people, the Angles?' said Oslaf. 'Where did they go?'

'Ah, to another land that once belonged to the Romans, a place across the Frisian Sea called Britannia,' said Widsith. 'Our northern neighbours the Jutes took part of it, and our southern neighbours the Saxons soon followed them. But we Angles have founded the biggest villages, and they are always growing. Elfritha has kin there, a powerful chieftain called Wuffa who would surely welcome the *Alfgaringas*.'

'Do you think Alfgar will ever do it?' said Oslaf. Widsith shrugged.

'There may come a time when he will have no choice,' he said, the red and yellow flames of the hearth-fire dancing in his milky-white eyes. 'Let us pray to Woden and Thunor and Friga that Alfgar will know the moment and not let it pass.'

It was warm in the hall, yet Oslaf suddenly felt cold, and shivered.

The next day Alfgar decided they should get on with the winter slaughtering, the time when the village's older and weaker animals were killed and the meat salted away for the hardest, coldest days ahead. He also ordered the stockade gate to be kept shut and barred day and night, and posted guards to keep watch. Oslaf and the other boys took their turn alongside the men, usually with a hearth-companion in charge.

The slaughterhouse was just inside the stockade, but the smell of blood seemed to hang over the whole village. At twilight one night, with the sun setting in a ball of fire to the west, Oslaf looked down from the fighting platform and saw a lean grey wolf staring up at him, its cold blue eyes like chips of ice. The wolf sniffed, clearly attracted by the blood-smell, and growled softly, showing its sharp teeth.

'Forgive us, Brother Wolf, but we have nothing to spare for you,' said Tovi, who was standing next to Oslaf. 'These are hard times for us all, man and beast.'

The wolf held their gaze for a moment longer, then loped away and slipped into the shadows. But the next night a whole pack paced and growled outside the stockade, and from then on they were constant visitors. People muttered, saying it showed how bad things must be – wolves never came so close to the village. Some even wondered if the beasts were truly wolves. Perhaps they were shape-shifting magicians sent to spy on the village and report back to the tribes heading towards them…

Widsith took that idea and made it into a poem he called 'Winter of the Wolves'.

Oslaf sat by him in the hall through the long, dark evenings, watching and listening as Widsith tested words and music until he was pleased with them. He even asked the old man if he could try his hand at the harp, and found it was hard to make it sing. But Widsith said he was good, and would get better with enough practice.

Then at dusk one evening, three days before the Yuletide Feast, the wolves didn't come as usual. Oslaf was on the fighting platform with Tovi and several others, men and boys. Tovi held up a flaming torch and peered at the lengthening shadows.

'Oslaf, go and tell Alfgar that we need everyone to be armed and ready,' Tovi said quietly. 'Something has scared off our grey brothers and sisters. I have a feeling in my blood that a different kind of wolf might be planning to visit us tonight.'

He was right. A little while later a war-band of armed men on horses came riding down the track. They yelled a wild war cry, a strange whooping from the back of the throat. Some threw torches once they were close enough, and others fired arrows. Oslaf ducked to let the feathered shafts fly over him. Alfgar stood with the rest of them, calling out orders, encouraging everybody. His helmet and chain mail gleamed in the light of the torches, and his sword shone like a flash of lightning in the dark. Oslaf thought he looked just like a hero from one of Widsith's warrior tales.

They threw their spears at anything that moved in the darkness, and managed to beat off the attack. Afterwards Oslaf couldn't stop shaking, amazed he had survived, unsure whether he had been any real help. When the sun rose they saw three men lying dead in front of the gates, spears sticking out of their chests. Oslaf suddenly felt sick, and decided he didn't want to know if any of the spears was the one he had thrown.

Alfgar spent most of that evening in his private chamber with Elfritha. Tovi and Beornath joined them, and everyone wondered what they were talking about.

Oddly enough, Oslaf the newcomer felt sure that he knew.

Everyone had been telling Oslaf for ages that the Yuletide Feast would be all eating and drinking and laughter, a dream of summer joy in the middle of the winter gloom. Yet it was a sombre gathering in Alfgar's hall that took place two days after the attack.

The chieftain stood tall and proud by the hearth-fire. The light of the flames glinted off the gold-rimmed bull's horn full of foaming mead in his hand.

'I welcome you to the last Yuletide Feast this hall will ever see,' he said. Oslaf heard a sharp intake of breath from the people around him, while others began to murmur, asking each other what Alfgar was talking about. 'There is nothing here for us any more,' Alfgar went on, raising his voice, and everyone fell silent again. 'We leave in the spring for a new land – for a new life in Britannia!' he roared.

He raised the bull's horn to toast their future, and the people roared back.

'To Britannia!' they cried out. 'To the next Yuletide in Britannia!'

Oslaf joined in, but his heart was full of fear.

What would this mean for him?

CHAPTER FIVE

Dark Red and Glistening

After Yuletide the village buzzed with excitement for a few days. The weather was cold but sunny, and people seemed happy at the prospect of leaving for a new life. Then the wind shifted, bringing snow from the north, and the mood changed. Oslaf heard people whispering to each other, their voices and faces now full of worry. A few even said they didn't need to leave, that things would get better soon.

'It is only to be expected,' said Widsith with a shrug one evening. He was sitting by the hearth-fire, Oslaf beside him as usual. Outside the wind howled like a giant beast, but it was warm and quiet in the hall. 'Sometimes even the bravest fear leaving the old and familiar for the new, although they know in their hearts it is the right thing to do. And then some of those who want to leave fear they will not be going.'

'What do you mean?' said Oslaf. 'Surely Alfgar will take everyone?'

Widsith snorted and shook his head. 'I'm afraid not, boy,' he said. 'There won't be enough room for everyone in the boats Alfgar will buy or build, and life will be hard in the new land. So Alfgar will take only those he can rely on – his family, his hearth-companions and their families, the best servants – oh, and me, of course.'

Suddenly Oslaf felt worried. He could see the sense in Widsith's words, but that didn't make them any easier to deal with. Why would a great chieftain such as Alfgar give a kinless boy like him a valuable place in one of his boats? There were many others in the village who were far more worthy. But then a thought occurred to him – perhaps he would have more of a chance if he made himself really useful...

From that moment on, Oslaf dedicated himself to being the best worker in the village. He got up before dawn every day and sought out Beornath so he could ask the steward what needed doing. He offered to do more guard duty, ran errands for Elfritha, did anything for anybody. Each night he fell exhausted into his sleeping place and knew no more till morning. But he was determined to keep it up.

One afternoon he was down at the pigpens, pouring feed for them into a trough, when Wermund and his followers walked by. Wermund saw him and stopped.

'I know what you're doing, Oslaf,' he said, smirking. 'You think that if my father hears what a good boy you are, then he'll be sure to take you to Britannia. Well, let me tell you something – you're wasting your time. It's me who is going to decide which boys come with us. And somehow I don't think you'll be one of them…'

Wermund walked off towards the hall with his followers. Oslaf watched them go, disappointment and anger boiling inside him, and wondered what to do. Then it came to him – why didn't he just ask Alfgar if Wermund spoke truly? Whatever the answer, at least he would know for certain – and he would be able to stop worrying.

Yet picking the right moment to speak to Alfgar was tricky. He was a difficult man to approach at the best of times, but he was busier than ever now, his mind clearly full of all that had to be done to get his tribe to Britannia. Oslaf thought of asking Gunnhild to speak to her father for him. The friendship between Oslaf and Gunnhild had grown, and Oslaf knew the chieftain rarely said no to his only daughter… But that was the coward's way, Oslaf realised. He had to do this himself.

He tracked Alfgar round the village for three days, but failed to pluck up the courage to speak on at least a dozen occasions. Then one morning he knew it was probably now or never. The chieftain was down by the main cattle pen, talking with Beornath and Tovi. There was no wind, but it was cold and their breath hung over them in a white cloud. A light dusting of snow lay on the ground and the puddles were frozen, so that they reflected the stone-grey sky. The men were wearing fur cloaks – Alfgar's was made from the pelt of a brown bear. Oslaf wore a thick woollen cloak Elfritha had given him.

'Lord Alfgar,' said Oslaf from behind them. 'May I ask you something?'

'I wish you would,' said Alfgar, turning to face him. 'I was beginning to wonder if I had somehow grown another shadow. Tell me what is on your mind, Oslaf.'

'I… I wish to know if I am coming to Britannia with you,' he blurted out.

'Why, of course you are.' Alfgar looked at him with a puzzled frown. 'You are one of us now, a true *Alfgaringa*. What made you think it would be otherwise?'

For the space of a few heartbeats Oslaf thought about telling him the truth, that it was Wermund who had put the idea in his head. But then he saw the truth of it – Wermund had simply been playing with him, tormenting him as a cat does a baby bird that has fallen from the nest. It was better not to show Alfgar he had been fooled.

'Nothing, Lord, just my own doubt,' he said at last. 'You have my thanks, and I promise I will do my best to serve you and the tribe as well as I can.'

'I know you will, Oslaf.' Alfgar smiled, and so did Beornath and Tovi.

They turned away from him, picking up their conversation where they had left it. Oslaf walked off, pleased there was certainty about his future. But that night, he dreamed of his mother. She was standing on the hillside where he had dug her grave, her arms outstretched, tears on her cheeks. He woke up sweating, his heart pounding, and remembered that he had promised to make a sacrifice to Woden for her.

In the morning he spoke to Elfritha, telling her about his promise. 'But Lady, I have no gold to buy an animal from Alfgar,' he said. 'Do you think he would let me have one I could pay for later? I will work even harder for him, I swear.'

'You work hard enough already, Oslaf,' she said. 'I will ask my husband if he will help you to keep your promise. And I think the tribe will need to make a sacrifice too. It would be a great mistake to leave behind us any spirits who are unhappy...'

A few days later the people of Alfgar's village walked in procession to a large glade in the woods. Alfgar led the way, and Beornath brought up the rear with a line of animals – a horse, a cow, a goat, a pig and a sheep. Oslaf walked with Widsith, the old man's big hand on his shoulder. In the middle of the glade lay a great slab of grey rock, its surface flat and covered with ancient, dark stains. Alfgar stood beside it, and the people looked on as he raised his arms to the blue sky above. He wore a whole wolf-skin, the muzzle covering most of his face and muffling his voice.

'Hear us, great Woden and Thunor,' he chanted as the people looked on. 'Hear us, spirits of the place where we have lived and died since before remembering. We give you these beasts in thanks, and beg you to wish us well as we cross the sea...'

Then the animals were brought forward one by one, and held steady by Beornath and several other men as Alfgar cut their throats, using the sacred *seax* that had been handed down from each chieftain to his son. He made sure the blood spurted on to the stone, and soon the slab was dark red and glistening, and the coppery smell of blood filled the glade. At last only the sheep was left, and Alfgar turned to Oslaf.

The chieftain held the handle of the sacred blade towards him. 'Take the *seax* now and make the sacrifice for your mother,' Alfgar said quietly. 'And ask her to look after the spirits of the dead, those of our kin we leave behind in our homeland.'

Oslaf felt Widsith give his shoulder a reassuring squeeze, and he stepped forward, taking the knife from Alfgar. Beornath and Tovi held the sheep down for him, Tovi pulling back

64

its head so its throat was ready for the blade. The creature's eyes rolled in fear, but then Tovi crooned softly in its ear and it seemed to grow calm. Tovi glanced up and nodded, and Oslaf made the sacrifice quickly and cleanly.

'Thus I keep my promise, Woden,' he said. 'Hear Alfgar's words, Mother.'

A sudden breeze rustled through the tops of the trees, and somehow Oslaf knew it was his mother speaking to him from the Land of the Dead, telling him she would do as Alfgar had asked. Oslaf raised his eyes to the sky and thanked her in his heart.

When he looked down again he saw Wermund staring at him with a mocking smile. Oslaf smiled back, and thought – *next time I won't be such a fool.* And he knew there definitely would be a next time. It was as if they were stuck in a war now, with neither of them able to back off or let their feelings go.

Oslaf had thwarted Wermund's wishes, and he was going to Britannia, so there was bound to be more trouble between them.

The days seemed to pass quickly from then on, which was strange in the deepest part of winter. This was when people usually stayed indoors as much as they could, and did as little as they could too. But the tribe was getting ready to leave and their days were full. They cleared out store cupboards and filled chests with the things they wanted to take with them to Britannia, and put food aside for the journey. Hard decisions were made – who would be left behind, what animals they would take with them or slaughter, and many more. Alfgar told the blacksmith he would have to leave his anvil behind – it was far too heavy to carry with them.

One day Alfgar rode to the coast with Tovi and his hearth-companions, and struck a deal with a seafaring tribe. They agreed to take the *Alfgaringas* across the Frisian Sea to Britannia in their boats. But it would cost most of the gold and silver coins and other treasure that Alfgar had inherited from his father and acquired himself.

Oslaf was curious about the place they were going to, and he soon made it his business to find out as much about it as he could. It seemed the Britons had not been totally defeated. They had fought hard for their land, and still held on to most of it.

'They nearly won too,' Widsith said. 'In the time of Alfgar's father, the Britons had a great leader called Artos who fought many battles against us. Artos died, and the Britons argued with each other – which made them easier to beat. But they are strong and cunning, and Alfgar will surely have to take the war-trail against them.'

Oslaf felt a thrill at the thought of Alfgar riding out with his hearth-companions against the Britons, and dreamed of being one of them. He was determined to become a warrior, to find a place that would always be his, no matter what happened.

A small voice deep inside him wondered if he would succeed.

CHAPTER SIX

Taking the Whale's Road

They set off on a cool, bright morning in early spring, a long column of people and ox-drawn wagons and herds and flocks all moving westwards. Alfgar rode at the front with Wermund and Tovi and a few of the hearth-companions, and the rest of them guarded the flanks and the rear. Elfritha and Gunnhild were in a wagon carrying the chests that contained the most important things from the hall, and Oslaf rode beside it.

At the top of the nearest hill he stopped to take one last look at the village. It already seemed small and distant and forlorn. The gates were wide open, and a few of the people who had been left behind stood watching the column as it moved away. Then a cloud passed over the sun and a shadow swallowed the hall and houses. Oslaf turned his back on the sight, and hurried to catch up with the rest of the tribe.

It took them ten days to reach the coast. They camped each night at dusk, forming the wagons into a defensive ring and making big fires for cooking and warmth. The weather stayed dry, and nothing much happened, except that an old woman died, a baby was born and three sheep were lost to wolves. When the column finally arrived at the coast, Widsith said it was a wonder they hadn't lost many more animals.

'We might lose plenty now though,' Beornath muttered. He and Tovi had gone with Alfgar to talk to the chieftain of the coastal tribe in his hut by the sea. 'The rogue is saying he wants our animals as well as the treasure or he won't let us use his boats.'

A long day crept past as Alfgar haggled with the sea-chieftain, and then another day, but on the third morning things were settled – Alfgar gave up the animals. But they couldn't have got them on the boats anyway – it turned out the sea-chieftain only had seven. As soon as he saw them, Oslaf knew that fitting in everyone and everything was going to be quite difficult. Each boat had twenty benches for the oarsmen provided by the sea-chieftain, and they took up a lot of the room on board.

The boats were drawn up on a long, windswept beach, and it took another day just to load them. At dawn the following morning the incoming tide lifted the boats off the sand and they finally got under way, the oars biting into the waves. Oslaf was in the leading boat, with Alfgar and his family and servants. The other boats were spread out behind, three on either side, and Oslaf found himself thinking again of the skeins of geese that flew south each autumn, honking their lonely farewell.

'Now I wander the waves, I take the whale's road,' Widsith murmured. He and Oslaf were standing in the stern of the boat, beside the steersman, one of the sea-chieftain's men. Widsith gripped the gunwale with both hands and raised his eyes to the sky, his hair streaming back in the breeze, his nostrils widening as he breathed deeply. 'Sea salt on my lips, a storm to come, sadness at journey's end…'

'Hush, Widsith, such words are dangerous!' said Oslaf. 'What if the Norns hear you? They might think that sounds like a good idea and make it our *wyrd*.'

'I'm sure the Norns listen to me all the time,' said Widsith, smiling. 'So they will know those words are from one of my poems, the "Tale of a Sad Seafarer".'

'Well then, you must tell me more of it,' said Oslaf. 'I like a good story.'

'It is a fine tale, though I say so myself.' Widsith's smile broadened into a wolfish grin. 'And don't worry, you will hear plenty of my tales on this voyage. I was a seafarer in my youth, and I know this journey will take many days, and also that there won't be much else for us to do… Although I was going to offer to teach you something of my craft. I have a feeling you might be interested to learn.'

Oslaf stared at Widsith for a moment, surprised yet again by the old man's ability to see into his heart. It was true – he had been thinking it would be good to learn how Widsith made his poems. They were such wonderful creations – words brilliantly strung together to make amazing pictures in your mind, gripping tales that drew you in until you were desperate to know what could possibly happen next.

'It is a fine offer,' Oslaf said as the sunlight sparkled on the waves and the boat skimmed the water like a leaping dolphin. 'And one I am happy to accept. I have a few stories I might be able to give you in return, tales my father told me.'

'Ah, I think we're going to get along very well on this voyage, Oslaf…'

The sea-chieftain's men kept the boats close to the coast as they voyaged to the west. Oslaf liked the comforting sight of land always being on their left. He had often gone fishing with his father, so he knew just how dangerous the open sea could be. He was also used to the rolling motion of boats, but others were not so lucky. They spent most of their time moaning, groaning and throwing up into the waves.

Then one morning, Oslaf woke to see that the land was gone. The sky was grey with clouds, the air was filled with a fine rain and the only sound was the splashing of oars as they dipped in and out of the water. Oslaf looked one way and another, but there was no sign of any coast – the sea and sky merged seamlessly together in the distance. He felt uneasy, and whispered a prayer to Woden under his breath.

'Fear not, Oslaf,' said a voice behind him. He glanced over his shoulder and saw that it was Alfgar. The chieftain was standing in the rear of the boat, beside the steersman, and smiled at him. 'The next coast we see will be Britannia…'

That moment came a while later, when a thin, smudged line appeared ahead of them. As they got closer, Oslaf saw tall cliffs with narrow rocky beaches below them. The sea-chieftain's men turned the ships northwards, following this new coast for another day and a night. They crossed a wide estuary, the mouth of a great river that led far into the west, and spent an uneasy night resting at anchor by the northern shore.

The next day a gusty wind blew from the east, chasing rags of cloud across a blue sky, and they arrived at their destination, a flat coastline where several streams and small rivers flowed into the sea. They rowed up the largest river, its banks thick with reeds, and Oslaf realised this too was a country of marshes, just like the Land of the Angles they had left behind. Eventually they came to a bend where the river widened into a deep pool. A long wooden quay had been built along the bank.

Alfgar gave the order to tie up the boats and jumped on to the quay, followed by everybody else. They were relieved to be on dry land, and for a while there was chaos as people filled the quay, the men throwing chests and boxes ashore, mothers chasing children. Oslaf stayed with Widsith, helping the old man off the boat – but then he felt a sudden strange prickling in his neck that made him look round.

A group of riders had appeared on the crest of a hill that rose beyond the river, the dark outlines of men and horses clear against the sky. As Oslaf watched, one man kicked his heels into his horse's sides and rode down the slope. A dozen more followed, and Oslaf saw now they were all armed, and their helmets and spear-tips and chain mail glinted in the sun. The sound of their horses' hooves was like thunder.

'Lord Alfgar!' Oslaf called out, pointing at the warriors heading their way.

'I know, Oslaf,' said Alfgar. 'It seems there is a welcoming party for us. With me, men!' he added, raising his voice. 'Get your weapons! Form a line here…'

The hearth-companions gathered round their lord, shields raised, spears at the ready. Wermund stood next to his father, the rest of the men and boys fanning out on either side, the women and small children behind. Oslaf was impressed by how quickly they all got organised, and noticed most of the women and girls had armed themselves with knives too. The sea-chieftain's men stayed in their boats.

Everyone fell silent as the riders halted just twenty paces from the shield-wall, their horses snorting and stamping. The leading rider nudged his mount forward, then stopped again and studied the *Alfgaringas,* his eyes moving slowly over the shields and spears, the people, the boats tied up behind them. Oslaf's heart pounded in his chest, and he wondered how Alfgar could stand there looking so calm.

'I am Breca, Lord Wuffa's coast warden,' the man said at last. 'What kind of strangers are you who come from the sea armed for war? Are you friends or enemies? You should know we are ready with the right welcome for you either way.'

Alfgar stepped through the shield-wall to face him. 'We are friends,' he said. 'I am Alfgar, son of Aldhelm, and we have come from Wuffa's ancestral homelands across the sea to settle here in Britannia. Wuffa is kin to my wife Elfritha.'

'Yes, Wuffa's father and mine were brothers,' said Elfritha, also stepping out of the shield-wall to stand beside her husband. 'So Lord Wuffa and I are cousins.'

'That may well be true,' said Breca with a shrug. 'But I cannot let you pass to Wuffa's hall unless you can prove that you are who you say.'

Now Alfgar looked angry, and a frown like a storm cloud passed over his face. But Elfritha put her hand on his arm and smiled up at Breca on his horse.

'I will send Wuffa a token, something of mine he will recognise,' she said.

Suddenly Oslaf saw a chance to serve Elfritha, and even perhaps gain a little glory. 'Let me be your messenger, Lady,' he said, stepping forward.

'But… but I should be the one who does that, not him…' said Wermund.

'Too late, my son,' said Alfgar. 'Oslaf spoke first, so the honour is his.'

Elfritha pulled a ring from her right hand, a silver band with a green stone. 'Show this to Wuffa,' she said, giving it to Oslaf. 'He will know it was passed down to me by our grandmother, and has been in our family since before remembering.'

Oslaf nodded and slipped the ring over one of his own fingers. He turned to Breca, expecting that he would have to climb the hill on foot. But the coast warden held out a hand, and Oslaf realised he would be riding to Wuffa's hall instead. He gripped Breca's forearm and the man hauled him up on to the horse's back. 'Hold tight,' said Breca, and Oslaf did just that as the horse turned and they galloped off.

The other riders followed, and they all went up the slope. Oslaf couldn't resist looking over his shoulder, searching for Wermund among the *Alfgaringas*. Wermund was staring, and even at a distance Oslaf could see the sheer fury in his face.

Oslaf smiled, then looked ahead as they rode over the crest of the hill.

CHAPTER SEVEN
A Bargain is Struck

I t turned out to be a short ride to the village of the *Wuffingas*, Lord Wuffa's tribe. His hall stood on another hill looking down across the river to the sea beyond. Like Alfgar's hall it was surrounded by houses, but there were far more, and the hall itself made Alfgar's seem small in Oslaf's memory. There was a timber stockade too, its gates guarded by a dozen warriors who waved Breca and his men through.

A huge bear of a man was standing before the carved doors of the hall, legs wide apart, hands on hips, a stern look on his broad, meaty face. He had a mane of black hair and a bushy beard that cascaded down over the front of his fine woollen tunic. A *seax* in a scarlet leather scabbard hung from his belt and hc wore two thick silver arm-rings, one above each elbow. Oslaf knew instantly this must be Wuffa.

'I bring a messenger from the boats that have arrived, Lord,' said Breca.

Oslaf jumped down from the horse and walked up to the chieftain. Wuffa stared at him, and Oslaf saw that his eyes were blue, the colour of warm summer skies.

'And I bring you a token from my lord's wife,' said Oslaf. He took the ring from his finger and handed it to Wuffa, who looked down at it nestling in his palm. Oslaf was about to say it was Elfritha's, and mention Alfgar, but there was no need.

'My grandmother's ring…' said Wuffa, and a giant smile spread across his face. 'Breca, go back and fetch Elfritha and her people up to the hall. We will show them that even in this new place we still keep to the old ways of welcoming kin.'

As Oslaf discovered, that mostly seemed to involve putting on a colossal feast. Wuffa was clearly delighted to see his cousin, and sat her and Alfgar and their children at the top table beside him and his wife Aelfgifu. There were places for the whole tribe at tables in the hall, and the evening passed in a haze of eating, drinking and singing. Wuffa had a *scop* of his own, but Widsith wasn't impressed.

'He sounds like a wildcat that's being strangled,' the old man muttered. 'In fact, someone *should* strangle him. It would be a great mercy for the rest of us.'

'Stop it, Widsith,' laughed Oslaf. 'You're just jealous because he's young.'

But Oslaf felt that Widsith was right. Wuffa's *scop* did have a poor voice, and he mangled the words. There should be a rhythm to a tale – four strong beats in every line, the sounds in each half of the line echoing each other. A good *scop* came up with clever ways to express things too, saying 'taking the whale's road' for setting out on a sea-journey, 'bone-house' instead of body, or 'enemy of wood' for fire. This man did none of that, and his tales were as flat and dull as a grey day in winter.

'Why don't you offer to take his place, Oslaf?' said Widsith. 'You're better than this wretch will ever be. I'd love to hear you tell that story about the monsters.'

Oslaf smiled. During their voyage to Britannia he had told Widsith the 'Tale of the Monsters from the Lake', as far as he could remember it, and Widsith had liked it very much. That wasn't really a surprise – Oslaf knew it was a wonderful story.

In the tale, the hall of the Danish king, Hrothgar, is attacked each night by a monster called Grendel. A young hero of the Geats called Beowulf comes to fight Grendel, and after a great struggle manages to wound him. Then the hero has to fight Grendel's mother, an even more powerful monster, and then there's a battle with a dragon. Widsith said Oslaf told the story well, but Oslaf wasn't so sure. He thought something was missing from his telling, although he didn't know what.

'No, I am no *scop*,' he said now. He didn't want to shame himself in front of Wuffa and Alfgar and everyone else by making a mess of the tale. He looked up and saw that Alfgar and Wuffa were deep in conversation, their heads together. 'You know everything, Widsith,' he said, changing the subject. 'What do you think will happen to us? Will Wuffa offer to settle the *Alfgaringas* here with his own people?'

'I doubt it,' said Widsith. 'It would be too many people to take into the village at once. Besides, Alfgar will want his own land, and I have a feeling Wuffa might just have a special place for the *Alfgaringas*. So there is a bargain to be struck.'

'But what can Alfgar give Wuffa? He has no treasure and no animals.'

Widsith smiled. 'Alfgar has the strength of his sword-arm, and good men to fight alongside him. Believe me, those things are worth a lot in a land such as this.'

Oslaf felt a sudden thrill at the thought of what might lie in the future.

The bargain was finally sealed a few days later, and Alfgar called all his people together outside Wuffa's hall to tell them what had been agreed. The *Alfgaringas* would have land to settle by a river north-west of Wuffa's village, a journey of three days on foot. Wuffa would help them build a hall and houses, and was giving them cattle, sheep and horses as well as seed so they could sow some crops.

Oslaf was standing with Widsith in the crowd. 'Lord Wuffa is very generous,' the poet muttered. 'That can only mean this place he is sending us to will be dangerous. I have a feeling things are going to be even livelier there than I thought.'

Widsith's words stuck in Oslaf's mind, and later that day he sought out Tovi. If anyone knew what they would be facing it was Alfgar's second in command.

'The old man is right,' said Tovi. 'We will be plugging a hole for Wuffa on the edge of the lands he rules. It is a weak spot for him, and his enemies know it.'

Those enemies were a real threat, it seemed. The local Britons regularly raided Wuffa's territory. They struck hard and fast, burning villages, stealing livestock, killing Wuffa's people, then quickly retreated to their strongholds. Wuffa sometimes caught them, and he did plenty of raiding himself, but he couldn't be everywhere at once. There had also been a lot of trouble with the Saxons to the south.

'So what was the point of coming here?' said Oslaf. 'It sounds just as bad as back home.'

'Ah, but we are part of something bigger now, Oslaf,' said Tovi. 'Wuffa is strong, and together with Alfgar he will be even stronger. Why, with two such chieftains fighting side by side, we Angles could take all of Britannia for ourselves.'

It was an amazing idea, and for a while Oslaf couldn't get it out of his mind. He would gain so much glory and honour if he played a part in such a great victory! Being kinless wouldn't matter any more – he would always have a place in Alfgar's war-band and by the hearth in his hall.

And perhaps one day *scops* would even tell tales about him, the mighty Oslaf, as they did about other great warriors…

But Oslaf's dreams quickly had to take second place to playing his part in another great effort, helping the tribe move to its new home. Alfgar led a party of men there, his hearth-companions and Wermund and some of Wuffa's best craftsmen. Oslaf begged to be taken along, and Alfgar gave in, much to Wermund's disgust. Nothing could dampen Oslaf's enthusiasm, though, not even Wermund's mockery.

They made camp on a low hill from where they could look down on the river. It was wide, and shallow enough to be crossed by a man on horseback. On the far bank were water meadows that probably flooded in the winter. Alfgar decided the best place to build his hall was on the crest of the hill, and they soon got started.

They worked through the spring and summer, through days of wind and rain and sun. The settlement was ready by the time the leaves on the trees were beginning to turn yellow in the early autumn. They had sown a crop of winter wheat, and they had plenty of salted meat stored away too. At last the rest of the *Alfgaringas* came in ox-drawn wagons, with Tovi and half the hearth-companions escorting them.

Oslaf was waiting at the gate of the stockade to welcome the new arrivals. It was the afternoon of a windy day, the sun playing hide-and-seek behind the clouds. He was pleased to see Widsith and Elfritha, and very pleased to see Gunnhild.

They smiled at each other, but then Oslaf noticed Tovi had ridden a little way off. The warrior was sitting on his horse, staring at something across the river.

'What is it, Tovi?' he asked, going over to him. 'You seem troubled.'

'We are being watched,' Tovi said quietly, and pointed with his spear.

Now Oslaf turned to look in the same direction. In the distance, three riders sat on their horses before a stand of trees. They wore helmets and long dark cloaks, and carried spears and blue-painted shields. As Oslaf watched, the rider in the middle pointed his spear back at Tovi. Then all three swung their horses round and passed into the shadows beneath the trees, vanishing as if they had never been there.

But they had, and suddenly Oslaf realised he had seen his first Britons.

Time passed, autumn turning to winter, then it was the tribe's first Yuletide in their new home. Spring followed, and a lovely summer that ended with a good harvest, and they all felt that things were going well. There were no raids, either, although it was clear the local Britons were keeping a close eye on them. Alfgar sent out regular patrols, and when they came back they always said they had been followed.

Oslaf made sure he pulled his weight, and worked just as hard as ever. He trained hard with the other boys too, and constantly pestered Tovi to let him go out on a patrol. But Tovi said such things were only for the hearth-companions.

'Very well,' said Oslaf. 'So when will I become a hearth-companion?' Training had just finished and Oslaf was helping Tovi to stack the spears and shields.

'And what makes you think you'll be good enough?' said Tovi, smiling.

'Everyone knows I'm a better fighter than all the other boys.'

'Not all of them, Oslaf. I think Wermund could still beat you.'

'That's only because he's a couple of years older than me,' said Oslaf. 'Wait until I have grown into my full strength. Then Wermund will see just what I can do.'

Tovi frowned. 'Let me give you some advice, Oslaf. Sometimes it is good to have a rival, a fellow warrior you can test yourself against. But you should never let it get out of hand – especially when your rival happens to be the son of your chieftain. Alfgar likes you, but Wermund is his firstborn son, his heir. Wermund is bound to be chieftain after his father, and he will remember those who challenged him.'

'I did not choose to be Wermund's rival. He started it, not me.'

'That may be so,' said Tovi with a shrug. 'But you should try to end it. Who knows, you might even be friends one day. Stranger things have happened.'

'I doubt it,' said Oslaf. But Tovi had certainly made him think…

CHAPTER EIGHT

Their Best War Gear

Oslaf soon decided Tovi might well be right about ending the rivalry with Wermund, and for a while he tried his best not to argue with the chieftain's son. That wasn't easy, as it only seemed to make Wermund much worse. Oslaf prayed often to Woden, asking the god to give him the strength to ignore Wermund's taunts. But it still wasn't enough, and things came to a head one cold autumn afternoon.

The boys were training, and when they had finished Tovi told them to stack their shields and spears as usual. Wermund muttered yet another insult about 'the kinless boy' – and Oslaf finally snapped. He flung himself at his tormentor, knocking him down. They grappled with each other, rolling through the mud, punching and gouging. A few of the others cheered, but most looked on in uncomfortable silence.

Tovi pushed through the crowd and grabbed Oslaf to pull him away. Oslaf kicked out at him, refusing to release his hold on Wermund. The warrior was too strong, however, and threw Oslaf to one side.

'That's enough!' Tovi yelled. 'In Thunor's name, what are you two fools playing at? Have you both lost your wits?'

'He hit me first,' said Wermund, slowly getting to his feet. His nose was bleeding, one eye was completely closed, and that side of his face was red and swollen.

'Only to make you shut up,' said Oslaf. He had a split lip and he could taste blood in his mouth. But he was pleased to see the damage he had done to Wermund.

Tovi sighed. 'How old are you, Wermund, seventeen summers?' he said. 'And you, Oslaf, fifteen summers? Well, you sound like a pair of babies who have only just learned to walk and talk. You deserve a good thrashing, and I'd be happy to do it myself. But I'll leave Alfgar to decide what your punishment should be.'

Alfgar was in the hall, sitting by the hearth-fire, talking and laughing with Elfritha. Gunnhild was sitting on a bench beside her mother, a piece of sewing in her lap. She smiled when she first saw Oslaf, but then she noticed the blood on his face and the state of his clothes, and her expression changed to one of concern. Tovi led Wermund and Oslaf up to the chieftain and quickly explained what had happened.

'Father, you should know that...' Wermund started to say when Tovi had finished. Alfgar turned to look at his son and scowled. Wermund stopped talking.

'All I need to know is that you have been too hard on Oslaf for too long,' said Alfgar, much to Oslaf's surprise. 'I should have done something about it before, but I thought it would pass, as these things between boys often do. You have a good heart, Wermund, and if you want men to follow you when you are chieftain, then you must learn to show them that as well as your strength. Do you understand?'

Wermund stared at him for a moment. 'Yes, Father,' he murmured at last, dark blood seeping from his nose. He wiped it away roughly with his sleeve.

'And as for you, Oslaf...' said Alfgar, shaking his head. 'You should have come to me, even though Wermund is my son. I am your chieftain, so it is for me to settle disputes and to keep the peace among my people. How can we fight our enemies if we are fighting each other? Believe me, the Britons are wolves who will sniff out any weakness within us and swiftly turn it to their advantage. Do *you* understand?'

'I... I do now, Lord,' spluttered Oslaf, and lowered his head, unable to bear Alfgar's gaze. He felt stupid and guilty and angry with himself, all at the same time.

'So, how shall I punish the pair of you?' said Alfgar. 'Elfritha, what do you think?'

'I think I ought to have done something about it myself,' said Elfritha, frowning at both boys. 'But now you should make them swear an oath to be friends.'

'An excellent suggestion,' Alfgar murmured, looking thoughtful. 'But if they are to go through all the trouble of swearing a solemn oath, then we might as well get the most out of it... I have it in my mind to make them hearth-companions.'

Oslaf raised his head. He could hardly believe what he had just heard – that was an even bigger surprise! Wermund also seemed startled by his father's words.

'Really?' said Elfritha. 'Surely they are a little young for such an honour.'

'They are young, but they are both ready,' said Alfgar. 'Do you agree, Tovi?'

'I do,' said Tovi. 'At least as far as their skills with weapons are concerned.'

'That is a good place to start,' said Alfgar. 'I have a feeling the tribe will need those skills before too long. And there is no better way to learn that we must trust each other or die than to stand side by side in the shield-wall. In *my* war-band we are shield-brothers, and we have no patience with childish feuds. Is that clear?'

'Er… yes, Lord,' said Oslaf. Alfgar nodded, then turned his gaze to his son.

'Yes, Father,' said Wermund, but Oslaf could see it cost him a great deal.

'Good,' said Alfgar. 'You can swear your oaths tomorrow. See to it, Tovi.'

At dawn the next morning the hearth-companions gathered in the large open space in front of Alfgar's hall. They were wearing their best war gear, and the bright sunlight glinted off helmets and chain mail and spear-blades. Oslaf and Wermund stood next to each other before the hall doors. Tovi had supplied them with helmets, proper chain-mail byrnies and spears from the tribe's store of weapons and armour. Alfgar had also given his son a beautiful Frankish sword, and a fine *seax* to Oslaf.

At last the hall doors opened and Alfgar came out. He too was dressed for war, his helmet topped with a tuft of boar's hair, his hand resting on the hilt of his sword.

Wermund took his oath first. He knelt before his father and spoke loudly and clearly so all could hear. 'I swear I will always do your bidding. I will fight to the death for you, and for my fellow hearth-companions, my shield-brothers…'

Then it was Oslaf's turn. He knelt and swore the same oath, making sure he spoke as clearly as Wermund. Alfgar smiled. 'I accept your oaths, and I swear to be a good lord to you,' he said. 'Men of the war-band, greet your new shield-brothers!'

The warriors behind Wermund and Oslaf roared their approval and banged spear-shafts and swords on shields. Oslaf turned round and saw that each and every one of them was grinning. Tovi winked, and at that moment Oslaf knew he should feel proud of what he had achieved. He did, of course – but he also felt a great sense of relief. He knew now that he should always have a place by the hearth in Alfgar's hall…

He silently offered thanks to Woden for keeping him on the right path, then glanced sideways at Wermund. Alfgar's son was smiling, but his face stiffened as he realised that Oslaf was looking at him. He met Oslaf's gaze briefly then turned away, and Oslaf wondered what he was thinking. Of course it was impossible to know.

They would just have to wait and see how things worked out between them.

Three days later Oslaf went on his first patrol. There had been reports of more Britons being seen west of the settlement, and Alfgar wanted to know if it was a war-band. So he sent a dozen men in that direction, with Tovi leading them. They were mounted, which was a little tricky for Oslaf. He could ride a horse well enough, but he had never before had to do it while wearing chain mail and carrying spear and shield.

Tovi soon spotted hoof prints in the mud on the far side of the river, and said he thought they had been made by a small scouting party, not a warband. They followed the trail and caught the Britons unawares in their camp by a wood – they barely had time to grab their weapons. Like Tovi and the others, Oslaf jumped off his horse to fight on foot. A Briton stepped forward, thrusting his spear at him. Oslaf deflected the blade with his shield and thrust back, only for the Briton to do the same.

They exchanged a few more thrusts, then the Briton turned and ran for his horse. The rest fled too, except for a couple Tovi had killed almost immediately. Oslaf looked at the bodies, the faces fixed in expressions of fear and shock, the blood dark against white skin. He felt his stomach churn, and for a moment he was sure he was going to be sick. But he kept his mouth shut and managed to hold it down.

'All right, Oslaf?' said Tovi. 'Just be glad it was them and not you.'

'I'm fine.' Oslaf suddenly realised it *could* have been him lying dead on the ground in a pool of his own blood. Then he did throw up, and Tovi laughed.

There were many more patrols that summer, and more fighting. The Britons raided villages to the north and south of the *Alfgaringas*, and one a day's ride to the east. Tovi said they were bound to get a visit from a war-band soon, and he was right.

The Britons came on a chilly autumn morning, charging out of the mist, screaming their war cries, shooting arrows, throwing spears and climbing the stockade wall. It was hot work on the fighting platform. Oslaf stood shoulder to shoulder with the other hearth-companions, jabbing his spear at the attackers, pushing them back, although some did manage to get through. Most of those were quickly killed on the fighting platform, but three jumped down and ran into the heart of the settlement.

Tovi leaped down too and went after them, Oslaf and Ragni following close behind. They quickly caught up with two of the Britons. Tovi threw his spear aside and drew his sword, and soon both Britons lay dead. The third made it as far as the open space outside the hall, but there he ran up against Elfritha and Gunnhild and the other women and girls. They were armed with wood-axes and spears and knives, and by the time Tovi arrived with Oslaf and Ragni they had the attacker surrounded.

Tovi pushed through the ring of women and girls. Oslaf and Ragni did too, and Oslaf saw that the Briton wasn't much older than Wermund. He was thin and dark and was wearing a leather jerkin with metal plates sewn on to it, plaid trousers tucked into boots and a round iron helmet. On his left arm he bore a blue-painted shield, and in his right hand he held a sword. His eyes were wild and he was panting.

'Drop your sword and no harm will come to you,' said Tovi. The Briton stared at him. 'Do you understand me?' Tovi added. 'I am offering to spare your life.'

'I can speak your filthy Saxon tongue,' the Briton snarled in a strange accent, spitting out the words. 'But I do not trust you whatever words you use.'

'Our tongues are alike, but we are not Saxons,' said Oslaf. 'We are Angles.'

'You are all the same to us – wild godless savages who came to take our land with fire and slaughter,' said the Briton. 'And we would rather die than give in!'

Then he ran at them, his sword raised. Without thinking, Oslaf moved forward to meet him as he had been taught, and rammed his spear into the Briton's chest.

Oslaf saw the light in the young man's eyes go out as he died.

CHAPTER NINE

Only the Strong Survive

The attack ended as quickly as it had begun, the raiders slipping back into the mist, leaving the *Alfgaringas* to count the cost. Five defenders were dead, and more were wounded, a few seriously. Oslaf had come through the fight unscathed, but that evening he couldn't stop shaking. Elfritha and Gunnhild were busy tending to the wounded, but they still found time to make him eat and drink. Gunnhild squeezed

Oslaf's hand, and that seemed to calm him a little. They both knew there was something special between them now, and he was glad to be with her.

Even so, he still slept badly that night, dreaming of the hatred on the young Briton's face. At last he rose from his sleeping place, intending to go for a walk to calm his mind. But he got no further than the hearth. Widsith was on his stool beside the fire, hunched over and wrapped in a thick fur cloak. 'Sit with me, Oslaf,' he said, and coughed. 'My old bone-house aches and my chest hurts, and I have need of your company.'

Oslaf pulled up another stool beside him. The two of them sat for a while without talking, Widsith coughing from time to time. 'I made my first kill today,' Oslaf said eventually. He stared into the yellow and red flames crackling and flickering in the big hearth. 'Tovi offered to spare a Briton's life, yet he chose to die.'

'Tovi is a wise man,' said Widsith. 'It is always useful to have a captive, someone we can exchange for any of our people who might be taken by our enemies. But it seems the Briton had courage. He was a true warrior and a worthy opponent.'

'I suppose so. But he said something that stuck in my mind. He called us godless, and I don't understand why. We have Woden, Thunor, Friga – plenty of gods.'

'Ah, but the Britons don't believe they are gods at all,' said Widsith. 'For them there is only one god, who died on a cross and came back to life. They call him the Christ, and themselves Christians. They worship their god in special buildings called churches, decorated inside with gold and silver and pictures – I have seen them myself. It is the same with all the lands once ruled by the Romans.'

'Well, good luck to them,' said Oslaf, sure Widsith was exaggerating again. 'But I don't see why they can't accept that we are entitled to have our own gods.'

'They hate everything about us, not just our gods. The Britons were part of something bigger once, and they cannot forget it. Rome ruled over a great Empire, but that has long since gone, and we came here to take what was theirs.'

'So we are to them as the tribes from the east were to us…' Oslaf thought of that first winter he had spent with the *Alfgaringas,* and the raiders who had attacked them. Now he felt he understood the hatred on the young Briton's face. But then hadn't Tovi also talked about the *Alfgaringas* being part of 'something bigger'? Did that mean the Angles too would be great for a time, and then lose everything?

'Such is the way of the world,' said Widsith. 'Only the strong survive. If your land is taken you must take another tribe's, or die, or live as slaves.' Suddenly he coughed and held his chest, his face pale. 'I grow weary, Oslaf. Take me to my bed.'

Oslaf helped Widsith to his feet and led him to his sleeping place. The old man lay down and closed his eyes, but he coughed again, and this time he couldn't seem to stop. Oslaf went to fetch Elfritha, who looked at Widsith and frowned.

'I didn't know things were so bad with you, Widsith,' she said, her voice gentle and soothing. 'Oslaf and I will stay by your side to take care of you...'

She turned to Oslaf, and his stomach almost turned inside out when he saw the worry in her eyes – she clearly thought Widsith might be very ill. It occurred to Oslaf that people often died of the coughing sickness, especially when they were as old as Widsith. Now Oslaf realised Widsith might have begun his spirit journey to the Land of the Dead. He gripped the old man's hand tightly, as if to hold him back...

Elfritha did all that she could, giving Widsith special potions made with herbs that sometimes helped people with such a sickness. But the old man's last breath came two days later, just as the sun was rising in the east. Oslaf wept until he felt empty, and stood dazed as Widsith was laid in his grave later that same day. He came to his senses long enough to ask for the *scop*'s harp before it was buried with him.

'Take it,' said Alfgar. 'I'm sure Widsith will find another in the Land of the Dead, and he would want you to have this one. The old man loved you like a son.'

And I loved him like a second father, thought Oslaf.

But he didn't say a word.

The raiding continued that summer, on both sides of the lands separating the Angles and the Britons. Oslaf quickly grew used to fighting off attacks at the settlement, and also to attacking the villages of the Britons. The days and nights were filled with fire and fury, the reek of smoke and blood, the crash of shields, the clang of blades, the screaming of men and horses. He killed again, and grew used to that too.

Alfgar's war-band did well, of course, never losing a fight, and it soon became famous. Men came to ask Alfgar if they could serve him – Angles from other settlements and villages, Saxons, Jutes from the lands beyond the great river, which Oslaf now knew was called Tamesis.

Alfgar accepted only the very best warriors among them, and turned the rest away. Even so, his war-band doubled in size.

Things quietened down after the harvest was in and the season changed, the hot weather giving way to a chilly autumn. Tovi said both sides needed time to lick their wounds and mourn for their dead. 'It is far from finished between our peoples, though,' he added. 'This is like a fire in the forest that seems to die, but flares up all over again a day or two later and burns even more fiercely than ever.'

The war-band was riding back to the village, Alfgar and Wermund at the head of the column, Oslaf and Tovi behind him. Tovi's words had made Oslaf think of the war between him and Alfgar's son. They had not argued since they had become hearth-companions, but neither had they spoken. In fact, they both went out of their way not to speak to each other. So perhaps their war wasn't finished either.

'You are right, Tovi, as always, and Wuffa agrees with you,' said Alfgar, looking over his shoulder. 'He has called the chieftains in his lands to a great feast in his hall, but I have a feeling there will be more talking than eating and drinking…'

They only had a few days at home in the village before Wuffa's feast. Oslaf missed Widsith, and whenever he went into the hall he still half expected to see the old man sitting on his stool by the hearth. But of course he wasn't, and that filled Oslaf with sadness once more. One night he sat on Widsith's stool himself, running his fingers across the strings of Widsith's harp, thinking of the songs the *scop* had sung.

Suddenly he felt a presence behind him, and he turned round. Gunnhild was there, her eyes and golden hair gleaming in the firelight. He smiled, the sadness inside him fading but not disappearing, and she smiled at him, her eyes shining now too.

'That sounds good,' she said. 'I would like to hear you tell a tale as well.'

'I am a warrior, not a *scop*,' he said, putting the harp aside. 'And this is a time for fighting, not for singing or telling stories. Perhaps that will change one day…'

'I hope so,' she said. She held his gaze for a moment, then walked away.

Oslaf watched her go, and he knew she had taken his heart with her.

Alfgar took only a few of his hearth-companions with him to Wuffa's village – Tovi, Ragni, Bebba, Wermund and, much to his amazement, Oslaf. He realised it was a great honour to be included, and he prayed to Woden, asking the god to make sure he brought no shame on himself or his lord. They set off on a cold autumn morning, the sky full of thick, dark clouds promising rain, and rode towards the east.

Three days later they arrived at Wuffa's village and found it buzzing with people. The chieftains of the Angles had already arrived, those of the North Folk and the South Folk, and like Alfgar they had each brought a few men with them. Alfgar and Tovi knew many of them, so there was much slapping of backs and laughter. At last Wuffa called them all into the hall, where Aelfgifu had set out the feast. They ate and drank, and the same *scop* as before told tales just as badly. Oslaf smiled, thinking of Widsith and his waspish tongue, and missed the old man all over again.

At last Wuffa rose to his feet and banged his drinking horn three times on the high table. The hall fell silent, everyone waiting to hear Wuffa speak his mind.

'I am a man of few words, and I have only one thing to ask you,' he said, his voice echoing in the hall. 'Is it not time that we broke the power of the Britons?'

'Yes, it is!' somebody called out. 'For too long we have suffered their raids!'

Others called out too, saying the same thing. Eventually Wuffa held up a hand and the hall fell silent again. 'Well then,' he said, smiling. 'It seems we need a plan…'

Wuffa spent the next day in his private chamber, talking with the most important chieftains. Alfgar was one, and Oslaf asked Tovi who the others were. Tovi named the chieftains of the Angles, but it seemed the Saxons had been invited too.

'I never thought I would see Wuffa in the same hall as Sledda of the East Saxons, let alone being friendly with him,' said Tovi, shaking his head. 'They were sworn enemies for years. Wuffa didn't much like Aelle of the South Saxons either. But here they all are, coming together at last to take on the Britons. I suppose they must have realised we have to fight side by side or risk being driven back into the sea.'

'Could the Britons do that?' said Oslaf. 'Surely they are not strong enough.'

'Anything is possible,' said Tovi. 'There have been rumours that the Britons are coming together as well. The men of Lindsey and Elmet in the north have been talking to the Britons of the west, those of Powys and Gwynedd. Perhaps their most important chieftains are somewhere at this very moment, settling their differences so they can attack us with a war-host bigger than this island has ever seen…'

It was a worrying thought, and suddenly Oslaf felt fearful for his home and its people, for Alfgar and Elfritha – and Gunnhild. He said more prayers to Woden, and to Thunor as well, begging the gods to guide the chieftains in their talking.

His prayers seemed to work, although Tovi seemed to think that it had been the good sense of Wuffa and Alfgar that did the trick. At any rate, it was agreed that the Angles and Saxons would fight as one war-host, with Wuffa as their leader.

'We will spend the winter preparing,' said Wuffa when they were all gathered in the hall once more. 'And we will strike in the spring. Death to our enemies!'

Oslaf cheered with the rest, and prayed to Thunor that they would win.

CHAPTER TEN

Red Dragon, White Dragon

T hat winter Oslaf often heard the sound of a hammer ringing on the blacksmith's brand-new iron anvil. Old weapons were repaired, new blades forged for spear-heads and battle-axes, dents in helmets were beaten out. Men fixed holes in their chain-mail byrnies with new links, or sewed new metal plates on to their leather jerkins. They checked the straps of their shields and replaced any that were frayed or loose.

The weather turned bitterly cold after Yuletide, and then it snowed, so there was a thick blanket of white covering everything. Oslaf hated the long evenings in the hall without Widsith there to tell his stories, and he began to feel that the spring might never come. But finally the snow melted and the days grew longer. One morning a skein of geese returning from the south flew over the settlement, honking joyfully.

'Not long to wait now, Oslaf,' said Tovi. The warrior was standing beside him outside Alfgar's hall, looking up at the birds. 'The call will come soon…'

Wuffa arrived the next day with five hundred men. They made camp on the far side of the river and Alfgar welcomed Wuffa into his hall, as he did the other chieftains when they came in the days after. Soon the war-host's camp was bigger than the whole settlement. A haze of blue smoke from their fires hung over it, and there was a constant buzz of noise – horses neighing, men calling out, laughing and singing.

Oslaf and Tovi stood looking at the camp from the settlement side of the river in the last rays of sunset. 'How many men are there in the war-host?' Oslaf asked.

'Five thousand, maybe more,' said Tovi. 'Good warriors as well, most of them, anyway. I only hope it will be enough. The Britons will have many men too.'

That evening a messenger rode into the settlement, a tall warrior on a white horse. Oslaf was standing outside the hall when he arrived, and knew immediately that the man was a Briton. Their warriors still wore Roman-style armour, short chain-mail tunics and round helmets with tall crests. The Britons were horse-warriors, their weapons a lance with a narrow blade and the *spatha,* a kind of longsword.

'I bring a message for Lord Wuffa,' said the warrior. He spoke the tongue of the Angles and Saxons with the same accent as the young man Oslaf had killed.

'You had better give it to me then,' said a deep voice. Oslaf turned and saw that Wuffa had come out of the hall, along with Alfgar and Tovi and the other chieftains. Tovi stood in front of the Briton, watching him closely, hand on his sword-hilt.

'The leaders of our war-host – Owain, High King of the West Britons, Maelgwn, Prince of Gwynedd, and Gwallog, Lord of Elmet – wish you to know that our god is the only true god, and that he will give us victory over you,' said the messenger. 'But we Britons have always been a merciful people. Leave our land now and we will let you go unharmed. We swear this in the name of Christ. What is your answer?'

'Our answer will be a storm of blades,' growled Wuffa. 'And we have no fear of your god. *Our* gods will give us the strength to break you once and for all.'

'So be it,' said the Briton, and he turned his horse to leave. Oslaf saw Tovi glance at Alfgar. The chieftain nodded, and Tovi stepped back to let the Briton pass. He rode out of the settlement, splashed across the river, and galloped westwards...

Two days later, on a bright spring morning, the war-host of the Angles and Saxons followed him. Wuffa rode at the head of the column with Alfgar and the other chieftains. Their hearth-companions were behind them, then a line of men marching on foot. At the rear were two dozen ox-drawn wagons. They carried the spare weapons and food, and there was a strong guard of mounted men to protect them.

Everyone else in the settlement – the women, children and the old – gathered to watch them go. Gunnhild stood beside Elfritha. As he rode past, Oslaf looked into her eyes and she smiled, although he saw with a pang that she had been crying.

He wondered if he would ever see her again.

Oslaf was half expecting to ride straight into a battle with the war-host of the Britons, but things turned out rather differently. For a start, all the Britons who lived near the lands of the Angles and Saxons seemed to have fled. Their villages were deserted, and Oslaf couldn't help thinking of the village he had seen on his way to ask Alfgar to take him in all those summers ago. Wuffa gave the order to burn the empty villages anyway.

They marched on, Wuffa sending out scouting parties, often led by Alfgar. He took Tovi, of course, along with a dozen of the hearth-companions, including Oslaf and Wermund. Several times they ran into small groups of mounted Britons and tried to make them fight. The Britons retreated as soon as they knew they had been seen, although they didn't seem in any particular rush to make their escape.

Alfgar was in no hurry to chase them either, and Oslaf asked him why. 'They are trying to tempt us into a trap, Oslaf,' said Alfgar. 'But we are not so foolish.'

At night they made camp, and moved on when the sun rose. On the third day they rode through a half-ruined Roman town. It was deserted, and Oslaf saw that the houses hadn't been occupied for a while. But many were big, and some did look as if gods might have lived in them. Oslaf wished now that he hadn't doubted Widsith and thought of what the old man had said about the *wyrd* of the Britons…

On the fifth morning they came to a grassy meadow with a hill beyond it. A dark forest stood to one side of the meadow, the undergrowth thick beneath the trees. The other side was bounded by a narrow river, its green water flowing swiftly between steep, rocky banks. It was a warm day, the sun shining in a blue sky and a soft breeze blowing from the south, ruffling the grass, rustling the leaves on the trees.

Wuffa held up a hand and the war-host halted. For a moment the only sounds were the snickering and snorting of the horses and the creaking of saddles. Then Oslaf heard the thunder of horses' hooves, or rather he felt it rising through the ground and his horse. He looked up in time to see the war-host of the Britons come galloping over the crest of the hill, their helmets and lance-points glinting in the sun.

'At last,' said Tovi, turning to Oslaf with a grin. His horse was eager for battle too, tossing its head and pawing the ground. 'Today will be the day of reckoning.'

Oslaf felt his stomach start churning in the familiar way. He had fought many times now, but there was always fear before any encounter with its prospect of pain and death. Besides, this fight was going to be far bigger than any he had been in before. The war-host of the Britons looked larger than that of the Angles and Saxons. For some reason they had stopped, and they covered almost the entire hilltop.

Orders were shouted by Wuffa and Alfgar, and for a while it was all noise and movement as the war-host got into position. But soon they were ready, the men on foot forming the shield-wall, flanked on either side by mounted warriors. Alfgar and his hearth-companions were on the right, with the forest beyond them. Wuffa sat on his horse behind the centre so he would have a good view of the battle.

Both war-hosts began to yell curses and insults at their opponents. Oslaf silently studied the Britons as he sat on his horse, and found himself thinking they looked much the same as the men around him. He could see their leaders, three warriors on horses behind the line. The Britons waved banners on long poles, most bearing the cross, the symbol of their god, but the biggest bore the scarlet image of a beast.

'It is a red dragon,' said Wermund. Oslaf looked round and saw that Wermund had moved his horse up to be by his side in the front rank. Only Alfgar and Tovi were ahead of them. 'My father once told me the Britons believe two giant dragons live in a great cave deep below a mountain in the west, one red and the other white. It is said that they fight day and night, and that their war will go on till one is dead.'

'Does the red dragon stand for the Britons, and the white for us?' said Oslaf.

'Perhaps,' said Wermund with a shrug, a strange look on his face. 'Or perhaps they stand for all those who cannot settle their feuds. Listen, Oslaf, I wanted…'

Suddenly there was a new noise, a whooshing sound, and the sky darkened with arrows fired by the Britons. 'Shields up!' Tovi yelled. Oslaf got his raised just in time, as an arrow thwacked into the wood, its barbed head punching through. Others were not so fast, and there were screams from men and horses who were hit. Wuffa's archers fired back, but then the Britons swept down the hill, their lances lowered.

'With me, men!' Alfgar called out, urging his horse forward up the slope to meet the Britons. His hearth-companions followed, among them Oslaf and Wermund. Oslaf's mind emptied of everything except the sound of his horse's hooves pounding on the ground and the sight of Alfgar and Tovi ahead and the Britons rushing down towards them. He gripped his horse with his knees and bellowed a war cry.

The Britons smashed into the hearth-companions. On both sides shields were splintered and men were flung from their saddles. A Briton jabbed his lance at Oslaf's face but he ducked, thrusting his own spear in return. Another Briton slashed at him with his *spatha* and Oslaf only just managed to take the blow on his shield. Soon he found himself trapped in a dense, struggling mass of flesh and sharp steel.

The noise around him was deafening – men were shouting, horses screaming, blades clanging.

Then his mount stumbled on something under its hooves, a body perhaps, and Oslaf was thrown headlong, losing his grip on both shield and spear. He crashed to the ground and lay stunned for a moment, the battle strangely distant now…

After a while he shook his head to clear it, and rose unsteadily to his feet. The fighting had moved on down the slope, leaving a trail of blood and death in its wake. The twisted bodies of warriors and horses lay around him, a few of the men groaning, a horse squealing horribly as it tried to stand. Then Oslaf saw something that made his own blood run cold. Alfgar was lying on his back, a lance sticking out of his chest, the shaft broken off halfway. Wermund was kneeling beside him.

Suddenly Oslaf heard the pounding of hooves. A Briton with a *spatha* was galloping his white horse up the slope towards Alfgar and Wermund. Oslaf cried out a warning, but Wermund didn't hear. So Oslaf ran in front of the Briton's horse, waving his arms and yelling as loudly as he could. The horse was startled and reared over him, pawing the air with its great hooves, the rider yanking at the reins, struggling to stay in the saddle and get his mount back under control.

Then the horse brought down its hooves and trampled Oslaf into the ground. After that there was only darkness shot through with pain, the most terrible pain...

CHAPTER ELEVEN
A Tale to Tell

For a long time Oslaf didn't know where he was. Strange flashes lit up the darkness and faces appeared, their mouths moving, saying words he didn't understand. There were strange visions too – his parents on the hillside above the farmhouse, reaching out to him, the seagull circling above. The young Briton he had killed coming back to life and attacking him, brushing his shield aside, slashing at him with his sword...

Oslaf woke with a shock and sat bolt upright, gasping for breath.

'Fear not, Oslaf, I am here,' said somebody, the voice calm and soothing. He felt an arm round his shoulders, and realised it was Elfritha. 'Drink this,' she said, holding a cup to his lips. His mouth filled with a warm, sweet liquid that had a tang to it.

He saw that he was in the private chamber of Alfgar and Elfritha, lying on their bed. Gunnhild was on the other side of the bed, smiling at him. Elfritha and Gunnhild helped him lean back against the headboard, but then the pain returned and he cried out. He looked down – his left leg was tightly bound with bandages from his groin to below the knee. It was throbbing, and the hurt was almost too much to bear.

Suddenly memories of the battle flooded into his mind and he gripped Elfritha's hand. 'Lord Alfgar…' he murmured. 'And Wermund, does he still live?'

'Alfgar is in the Land of the Dead,' Elfritha said, and now Oslaf noticed the dark rings like bruises under her eyes and heard the sadness in her voice. 'Wermund lives, and he and Tovi and the others brought Alfgar home. We raised a mound of earth to make a tomb fitting for a great chieftain, and buried my husband in it three days ago. Then we proclaimed Wermund chieftain, as his father would have wanted.'

'Three days ago?' said Oslaf, confused. 'But… how long have I been asleep? And what about the battle? Did we beat the Britons? Tell me, I have to know!'

'Calm yourself, Oslaf,' Gunnhild said softly. 'We will bring you food now you are awake at last, and while you eat we will tell you everything that happened…'

When the food arrived – a bowl of stew and some crusty bread – Oslaf realised he was starving and he ate ravenously, listening to Elfritha and Gunnhild. He was relieved to find out the Angles and Saxons had been victorious, and proud when he heard why. If Alfgar hadn't ordered his men up the hill to meet the Britons, the enemy would almost certainly have destroyed Wuffa's war-host, like a wave sweeping all before it. As it was, they were broken on the rock of the hearth-companions.

But the Britons were tough and stubborn, and the fight had gone on for some time. Eventually Wuffa had led the war-host to the top of the hill and driven them off. They had left hundreds of their men dead on the battlefield, and had pulled back deeper into their own lands. The war wasn't finished yet, though – it seemed Wuffa was sure there would be another battle before long, with the Britons turning like a stag at bay.

'Not too soon, I hope,' said Oslaf, wiping the bowl with the last of the bread. The pain in his leg had receded a little, perhaps because his stomach was full now, or more likely because of the drink Elfritha had given him. 'I want to be at that battle so I can take vengeance for Alfgar. When will I be able to ride and fight?'

Gunnhild looked at her mother. Elfritha took Oslaf's right hand in both of hers. 'I am sorry to tell you this, Oslaf,' Elfritha said, her voice gentle. 'In time you might be able to ride again, at least after a fashion. But your fighting days are over.'

It felt to Oslaf as if all the air had instantly been sucked out of his lungs.

'What… what do you mean?' he said, staring at her. She held his gaze.

'Your thigh-bone was broken and your knee smashed,' she said. 'I have set the bone and done everything I can for your knee, but I do not think it will ever be as it was before. You will limp for the rest of your days, perhaps quite badly…'

She said more, but Oslaf stopped listening. He wanted to argue, to shout and scream and tell her she couldn't possibly be right. But everyone in the tribe trusted her judgement in such matters. So if the Lady Elfritha said he would never be a warrior again, he knew he should accept it. And just like that, in the space of a few heartbeats, he felt the life he had built for himself begin to crumble into dust.

'Leave me,' he said. He lay down and pulled a blanket over his head.

Then he closed his eyes and burrowed deep into the darkness inside.

Spring turned into summer at the settlement of the *Alfgaringas*, as they still called themselves, even though Alfgar lay in his mound. Oslaf slowly got better, the pain in his leg fading. There were some bad days, and for a while in the hottest part of the summer he had a fever that kept him in bed and gave him strange visions again. But by autumn he could walk, although he needed the help of a wooden staff.

Wermund and Tovi and the other men had returned to the war-host after Alfgar's funeral. News came of them from time to time – there was another battle, the Britons were pushed westwards even more, but they still refused to give up. Then one chilly, rainy day Wermund and the rest of the hearth-companions rode into the settlement. Both sides were exhausted and had agreed there would be no more fighting until next spring.

That winter, as the nights grew longer and the days darker, Oslaf sank into a deep gloom. He rarely spoke, not even to Gunnhild, preferring to sit in silence on Widsith's old stool by the hearth-fire, looking into the flames, brooding on how things might have been. One afternoon, Wermund pulled up a stool and sat down on the other side of the hearth from him. Apart from the two of them the hall seemed empty.

'Don't worry, Wermund,' said Oslaf. 'I can save you the bother of telling me I don't have a place here any more. I will leave tomorrow and never return.'

'Is that what you think I want?' Wermund met his gaze across the flames.

'Of course! You have hated me from the day we first met and never wanted me here. It was your father who took me in. But now you are chieftain of the tribe, you can finally throw me out.'

'I'm sorry, Oslaf, you are wrong. I am here to thank you for saving my life. And I wanted to ask why you did it. You are right, I have never been a friend to you.'

Oslaf had wondered about that himself, but now he knew the answer. 'I swore I would fight to the death for your father... and my shield-brothers,' he said with a shrug.

'I swore the same oath, and now I see what it truly means,' said Wermund. 'I am sorry for how I treated you in the past, Oslaf. You are one of us, and you will always have a place by my hearth. I only hope you can forgive me for everything…'

'Forgiving you is easy,' Oslaf said. 'But I will not stay if I cannot be of use to the tribe. I can't be a warrior now, so what else can I do? I will just be what I was to begin with – another useless mouth to feed. No, I will leave tomorrow.'

Wermund spoke again, trying to make him change his mind, but Oslaf refused to listen or even look at him. Eventually Wermund gave up and left him alone.

'He was telling the truth, Oslaf,' someone said. He looked round and Gunnhild came out of the shadows. 'None of us wants you to leave… especially me.'

'But what can I do?' he said. 'You know I would rather die than sit idle while others work or fight. I cannot do that… it just wouldn't be right or fair.' His eyes filled with tears, and he turned away from her so she wouldn't see.

'There is something you can do,' she said. 'You can be our *scop*.'

Oslaf shook his head. 'I am too young to be a *scop*, and I would never be good enough. A *scop* needs to have lived long and seen and done many things.'

'No, you're wrong. Widsith thought you were good enough already. In fact he was always telling everyone you were much better than he was at your age.'

'Did he?' Oslaf was surprised and pleased. Maybe the idea wasn't so impossible then. If Widsith had believed in him, perhaps he should believe in himself...

Later that day he went to retrieve Widsith's harp. He had put it away in an old wooden chest to keep it safe when he had gone to fight the Britons. The harp was a little out of tune, but fine otherwise, and seemed to come alive, twanging when he ran his fingers lightly over the strings. He thought about the wonderful stories Widsith had told in his spellbinding way, and realised he knew most of them by heart.

Then it occurred to him that he knew quite a few other stories too, the tales of the Geats his father had taught him. Widsith had said the 'Tale of the Monsters from the Lake' was one of the best stories he had ever heard. Suddenly he heard Woden's voice in his mind once more – or was it the voice of Widsith? *It is your fate to be a scop, Oslaf, your wyrd*, he said. *And a hall needs a scop as much as it needs a hearth-fire…*

Oslaf went off to find a quiet place where he could practise alone.

Five days later, on the longest night of the year, the people of the settlement gathered in the hall – Wermund's hall now – for the Yuletide feast. Outside a cold wind howled, bringing sleet and snow from the north. But inside there was warmth and light, the hearth-fire burning brightly, and plenty of food and drink and talk and laughter. There were tears and sadness too, as toasts were made in memory of all those who had died.

After a time Oslaf rose from the bench where he had been sitting with Gunnhild and Elfritha and Wermund, and went to sit on Widsith's stool by the hearth.

'Quiet, everyone!' Wermund yelled, and an expectant silence fell in the hall.

Oslaf looked at all the faces, his eyes coming to rest at last on Gunnhild, her golden hair shining in the firelight. She smiled at him and he smiled back, although he felt almost as sick with fear as he had done before the battle with the Britons.

'I will start with a story my father told me,' he said. 'The Tale of Beowulf.'

He took a deep breath, let it out, and boldly struck the opening chord.

Listen! I sing of Spear-Danes and doom in
days gone past,
Of grim Kings and great deeds, of death and
gore,
Of monsters and mayhem, a young man of
courage...

The silence in the hall seemed to deepen and everyone leaned forward to listen, so Oslaf knew he had them gripped. He realised he was telling the story well, better than he had ever told it before. Perhaps it was because he had been through so much himself. Now, when he sang of fear and triumph, happiness and grief, he understood just how those things felt – and that they all passed, or became something else.

He finished the tale at last, and the hall was filled with cheers and people calling out his name. Wermund stood and raised his drinking horn to him in salute.

'I give you Oslaf, our new *scop*!' he roared. 'Here's to his next tale!'

Oslaf smiled. He did have another wonderful tale to tell, the story of a kinless boy who found a new family and went with them to build a home in a new land.

He struck an even bolder opening chord on the harp, and started to tell it.

Historical Note

Britain was part of the Roman Empire for nearly four hundred years. The original Celtic inhabitants had their own culture and language, but had gradually become very Romanised, particularly in southern and eastern Britain. Many of them probably spoke Latin, the language of the Romans, as well as their own tongue. They had also given up their gods and become Christians, along with most of the Empire.

However, during the fourth and fifth centuries, the Roman Empire faced many problems, and was being invaded by tribes from beyond its borders. By the end of the fifth century the Empire – at least in its western part – had completely collapsed, and the invaders began to carve their own lands out of its remains. The peoples who came to Britain were originally from the part of Europe we now know as northern Germany and Denmark. They were called the Angles and the Saxons, and it was said their original homelands remained almost empty of people for years after they left.

This period of history in Britain is something of a dark time. There are few written records of what happened, but quite a few legends. We do know that the Britons fought the Angles and Saxons for centuries, but were pushed westwards, into Wales – 'Wales' is actually the Anglo-Saxon word for 'foreigners'. People in Wales still speak Welsh, the language descended from the original tongue of the Britons. The language of the Angles and Saxons eventually became English. It was very different at that time, more like German, but we still use many of the same words today.

The Angles settled in the east of the country, which is why we now call it East Anglia. They were divided into the 'north folk' and the 'south folk' – which is where the names 'Norfolk' and 'Suffolk' come from. The East Saxons and the South Saxons gave their names – Essex, Sussex – to the lands they settled. Wessex – the land of the West Saxons – became the strongest kingdom. Its most famous king was Alfred the Great, and he defeated another wave of invaders, the Vikings. Alfred's grandson Athelstan was the first king of the whole of Angle-Land – or England as we now know it.

The Romans generally thought of peoples such as the Angles and Saxons as savage 'barbarians', but the ancestors of the English had a rich culture. They had their own gods – Woden, Thunor and Friga, among others. The names are similar to those of the Viking gods, Odin, Thor and Freya. The Vikings came from lands close to where the Angles and Saxons had been living, and the Viking language – Norse – was also very much like that of the Angles and Saxons.

The Angles and Saxons loved riddles, wordplay and poetry. We know that because quite a few of their poems have survived. Some are about battles ('The Battle of Maldon'), others are about voyages across the sea ('The Seafarer'), and one is about the remains of a Roman town ('The Ruin'). The greatest is 'Beowulf', the tale of a hero who fights three monsters. Reading these poems today – even in translation – helps us to understand how the people of those times thought about their lives.

The story of Beowulf was probably first told before the Angles and Saxons came to Britain. Beowulf is said to be a hero of the Geats, a tribe known to have lived in southern Sweden, and he helps Hrothgar, King of the Danes. It may well have been a legend, an ancient tale that people liked to hear being recited by a poet – a *scop* – on long winter evenings in the hall of their chieftain. Over the years other poets then told versions of the story, making it their own, adding and changing things.

I've always loved the poem – it's exciting and scary, but full of sadness too. So I wondered how it might have come to these shores, and that led me to create the character of Oslaf. Another poem to have survived is called 'Widsith', and that gave me Oslaf's mentor – although the original Widsith was pretty big-headed. Wuffa was the legendary founder of East Anglia, and was said to be the ancestor of the seventh-century King Raedwald, probably the man buried with his incredible treasure at Sutton Hoo in East Anglia. There were also connections between Raedwald and southern Sweden.

So it all seemed to fit, and I simply had to weave it together, as Widsith might have done. Somehow I don't think the art of telling a story has changed much over the centuries. I hope you enjoyed reading Oslaf's story as much as I did writing it...

GLOSSARY

Angles   a Germanic people from the
                  part of Europe we now know
                  as northern Germany and
                  Denmark, who arrived in Britain
                  in the fifth century CE

Britannia   the Roman name for Britain

Britons   people who lived in Britain
                  before the arrival of the
                  Anglo-Saxons

byrnie   a piece of chain-mail armour
                  that covered a soldier's neck
                  and shoulders

Elmet   a small ancient kingdom roughly
                  corresponding to part of Yorkshire
                  today

Franks	a Germanic tribe who took over Gaul as Roman rule ended
Friga	goddess of love and wisdom and wife of the god Woden in Anglo-Saxon mythology. In Norse mythology she is known as Freya.
Frisian Sea	an area of the North Sea near to what is now the Netherlands
Gaul	the Roman name for a land that today includes France and parts of some of its neighbours
Geats	a Germanic tribe from Scandinavia
Goths	a Germanic people from Scandinavia who took over most of Hispania as Roman rule ended
Gwynedd	an ancient Welsh kingdom, today a county in Wales
hand-fasted	engaged or married
Hispania	the Roman name for what is now Spain and Portugal

Jutes	a Germanic people who invaded Britain in the fifth century CE along with the Angles and Saxons
Lindsey	a small ancient kingdom roughly corresponding to part of Lincolnshire today
mead	an alcoholic drink made from honey, water and spices
Norns	legendary figures who create and control fate
pelt	animal skin or fur
pommel	the knob at the top of a sword or dagger
poultice	a treatment for wounds and swellings, made from a heated mixture spread on a cloth or spiders' webs
Powys	an ancient Welsh kingdom, today a county in Wales
Saxons	a Germanic people from the part of Europe we now know as northern Germany and Denmark,

	who arrived in Britain in the fifth century CE
scop	a court poet
seax	a long knife or dagger used by the Anglo-Saxons
spatha	a type of long, straight sword
stockade	a defensive wall built of large wooden posts
Tamesis	the Roman name for the river Thames
Thunor	god of thunder in Anglo-Saxon mythology. In Norse mythology he is known as Thor.
Vandals	a Germanic tribe who are famous for attacking and destroying Rome
Vikings	people from Scandinavia who settled in parts of the British Isles from the eighth century CE. They are also known as Norse people.
Woden	king of the gods in Anglo-Saxon mythology. In Norse mythology he is known as Odin.

wyrd	fate, a power that decides everything that happens, according to Anglo-Saxon belief
Yggdrasil	the mighty tree that supports the whole universe in Anglo-Saxon and Norse mythology
Yuletide	a midwinter festival celebrated by Anglo-Saxons and other ancient northern European peoples. Some of the Yuletide customs have been kept as part of Christmas traditions.

Also by
TONY BRADMAN

ISBN: 9781472929327

Marcus is excited about travelling to Britannia, the island at the edge of the world. But the Britons are savages who tattoo themselves and take the heads of their enemies in battle, and won't bow down to the rule of Rome. As this young Roman travels to meet his father his destiny is changed forever, along with that of Britannia...

Also by
TONY BRADMAN

ISBN: 9781472929402

Finn wants to be a Viking, and seek adventure
and glory in far-off lands, not be a village
chieftain like his father. But when his father is
called away, Finn is left in charge, and danger
strikes. Can Finn save the day and learn what it
really means to have the blood of a Viking?